THE UNKNOWN
ZONE

THE INCREDIBLE SPACE RAIDERS FROM SPACE!

THE INCREDIBLE SPACE RAIDERS FROM SPACE!

WESLEY KING

A PAULA WISEMAN BOOK
Simon & Schuster Books for Young Readers
New York London Toronto Sydney New Delhi

SIMON & SCHUSTER BOOKS FOR YOUNG READERS
An imprint of Simon & Schuster Children's Publishing Division
1230 Avenue of the Americas, New York, New York 10020
This book is a work of fiction. Any references to historical events, real people, or real places are used fictitiously. Other names, characters, places, and events are products of the author's imagination, and any resemblance to actual events or places or persons, living or dead, is entirely coincidental.

Jacket design by Laurent Linn
Interior design by Hilary Zarycky
Endpaper art by Orlin Culture Shop
The text for this book is set in Minister.
Manufactured in the United States of America
0115 FFG
2 4 6 8 10 9 7 5 3 1
Library of Congress Cataloging-in-Publication Data:
King, Wesley.
The Incredible Space Raiders from space! / Wesley King.—First edition.
pages cm
"A Paula Wiseman Book."
Summary: In 2156, when Jonah awakens on the *Fantastic Flying Squirrel*, he is informed that he is one of 200 children being trained as The Incredible Space Raiders, whose mission is to destroy the Entirely Evil Things of the Dark Zone, but there is more going on than any of the children could guess.
ISBN 978-1-4814-2319-9 (hardcover)—ISBN 978-1-4814-2321-2 (ebook)
[1. Adventure and adventurers--Fiction. 2. Heroes—Fiction. 3. Space flight—Fiction. 4. Orphans—Fiction. 5. Humorous stories. 6. Science fiction.] I. Title.
PZ7.K58922Inc 2015
[Fic]—dc23
2014010044

For Samantha Goodwin,

The Bravest and Most Daring Adventurer

CHAPTER ONE

JONAH BLINKED SEVERAL TIMES BEFORE HE realized she was not going away. He took one last extra-long blink, just to be sure, and then opened his eyes. Still there.

"Ready to wake up yet?" she asked politely.

"No," he replied.

She smiled and nodded. "Okay. I can wait."

Jonah frowned and looked around the room. It was small and mostly empty, apart from a cot tucked against the wall. The walls themselves were made of rusty-looking gray metal, and a few dim light panels flickered on the ceiling, casting everything in an eerie white glow. Jonah wondered why he was sitting on the floor. It was hard and cold.

When he finally turned back to the girl, she was still just smiling patiently and staring at him like he was a new pet. She seemed a little odd.

For one, she was wearing what could only be described as a uniform. It was a faded brown color and far too big, but it had a belt and a black patch sewn onto the chest.

The patch said ISR in red letters. That was strange enough for someone who must have been about eleven years old. But she also had on a pair of broken glasses, was wearing bright red lipstick, and had wild brown hair tied up in bunches, like a porcupine having a bad hair day.

"Who are you?" Jonah asked.

She stood at attention and saluted. "Willona the Awesome, at your service."

Jonah raised his eyebrows. "Your name is Willona the Awesome?"

"Exactly."

Jonah looked around the room again. "And where am I?"

"The *Fantastic Flying Squirrel*."

Jonah rubbed his forehead. "The what?"

"The *Fantastic Flying*—"

"I heard you," Jonah said quickly. "Why am I here?"

Willona smiled happily. "Because you have been specially selected to join the Incredible Space Raiders from Space. You should be honored. There were only two hundred members chosen from the entire solar system. And you were the last! The extra-special recruit. That's why we gave you such a good room."

Jonah looked around. "This is a good room?"

Willona shrugged and gestured behind him. "Well, you got a window."

Jonah slowly turned around. His eyes widened.

He wasn't leaning against a wall. It was a window. The

reflection of a small, skinny boy with a mop of messy hair and bright green eyes was staring back at him. Behind that reflection, and behind a few inches of extra-thick glass, was outer space.

And sitting in that, now small in the distance, was the familiar blue-and-green ball that was Earth, where his big white-bricked home with a long black driveway and neatly trimmed lawn stood at the end of Eleventh Drive.

Jonah stared out the window for a moment and then turned back to Willona.

"What is the *Fantastic Flying Squirrel*?" he whispered.

Willona smiled. "Come with me."

Willona led Jonah down a long hallway made of the same dark-gray metal as the room he'd woken up in. Dusty old light panels ran along the ceiling, and most of them were flickering ominously or out altogether. Large steel double doors with black-and-yellow stripes blocked the hallway farther ahead. There was no plush carpet or nice pictures or anything else Jonah was used to seeing in hallways on Earth—just identical gray doors lining both walls, all with little grooves for handles. There were lots of those.

As they walked, kids in overlarge brown uniforms kept marching by or popping out of open doorways. Every one of them grinned at Jonah and saluted crisply.

They looked normal enough, besides the uniforms and the fact that many were holding long metal pipes like

like weapons. They were all kids, the oldest only about fifteen years old. Most were wearing ratty old sneakers, but a few had no shoes at all.

"This hallway is called Squirrel Street," Willona said, gesturing around them. "It's where every Space Raider lives. But you see those big double doors with the warning stripes? Squirrel Street continues on the other side of it, but we can't go there unless ordered by a lieutenant or the commander, because that's the next sector—there are four sectors total. This is Sector Three. It's clearly the best sector, which is probably why they put me here."

Jonah felt he should sit down. She patted one of the identical gray doors.

"Most of these doors lead to bedrooms like yours, but we also have bathrooms and, of course, a cafeteria—one for each sector." She glanced back. "Are you all right?"

Jonah shook his head. "No."

"That's okay," she said. "It's a lot to take in."

It wasn't the fact that they were in space that was so perplexing to Jonah. In the year 2156, space travel was fairly common. Humans had overpopulated Earth fifty years ago, and they now also lived in domed colonies all across the solar system. There was even a colony on icy Pluto. Jonah had never been on a spaceship before, but his parents had.

What was confusing was that the only people he had seen on this ship were children, and they were marching around like they were the crew. That had to be illega

"Where are the adults?" Jonah asked.

Willona laughed and kept walking. "Adults? The ISR doesn't need adults."

Jonah frowned as a boy with red hair saluted and walked by.

"Who are you people?"

"Ah," Willona said, "I should probably explain."

She stopped in the middle of the hallway and pulled a notepad out of her uniform pocket. Adjusting her glasses—even though there were no lenses—she turned to the first page and started reading.

"'Welcome, recruit. You're probably wondering where you are.'" She looked up and smiled. "I really should start with this."

Willona continued reading.

"'Four years ago scientists on Earth made a groundbreaking discovery. They found new life.'"

"I never heard about that," Jonah said.

She glanced up at him. "May I continue?"

"Sorry," Jonah murmured.

"'There was just one problem: The life they found was not friendly. They called them the Entirely Evil Things—or the EETs. The EETs come from a starless part of our galaxy called the Dark Zone. The scientists observed black ships flying out of the Dark Zone, and whenever the EETs found a habitable planet, they landed and proceeded to consume all life. Earth sent a ship to the Dark Zone to make contact, but they never heard from it again. Since then, we've stopped trying to talk.'"

Jonah didn't like where this was going.

"'On that day, Earth came up with a new plan. The Incredible Space Raiders'—that's us—'were selected to travel to the Dark Zone and destroy the Entirely Evil Things.'"

Jonah paled. "But we're just kids."

"Exactly," Willona said, looking up. "The EETs prey on our weaknesses—our fears and mistakes and worries. An adult has too many. And so the ISR is made up entirely of children: those pure of heart and full of noble intention."

She returned to her notes.

"'If we don't stop them, the Entirely Evil Things will spread across the universe, consuming everything in their path. And so you, noble recruit, are now officially a member of Earth's last defense, and you are tasked with saving humanity from evil.'"

Willona closed the notepad and met Jonah's eyes.

"And that is not the only danger we face," she whispered, looking around the hallway. "The *Squirrel* is home to two other forces of evil. The first is Captain White Shark and his crew. They were hired by Earth to take us to the Dark Zone, because only a crew so evil could ever survive there. There are rumors that they kill Space

Raiders for fun. Not sure if it's true, but I wouldn't be surprised."

Jonah felt his knees wobbling.

Willona leaned in. "But that's not the worst thing on this ship."

"It's not?" Jonah murmured.

She shook her head. "We call it the Shrieker. It roams the hallways, coming and going like a shadow. You'll hear it in your sleep. What is it? We don't know. A ghost, maybe. An alien creature. A monster. But it's not human, we know that. And it preys on Space Raiders who venture outside the safety of Squirrel Street."

Willona stood up straight.

"This is a dangerous ship. But we are Space Raiders, and our only job is to survive long enough to get to the Dark Zone and save the universe from evil. Do you accept your noble task?"

"Well—," Jonah said.

"Excellent," Willona cut in. "Shall we?"

She continued marching down the hallway, and Jonah hurried to catch up. They walked past a second, smaller hallway that joined up with Squirrel Street. Gathered at the entrance to the hallway were ten Space Raiders standing in front of a tall boy with dark hair and serious brown eyes. He was giving them a lesson.

"The EETs are big," he said, "but they have trouble hitting a moving target. You have to be fast, and when the time comes you have to attack even faster."

He started swinging his metal pipe back and forth in a complex pattern, and then he suddenly lunged forward, stabbing at an invisible enemy, shouting, "Take that, fiend!" As he did, the other Space Raiders followed him in perfect synchronization. They looked very impressive.

For just a second, Jonah thought it might be nice to be on a team. He'd never been on one before, other than the Science Club, and they definitely didn't get to use weapons, unless you counted the time Jonah's experiment blew up and turned his partner's face green. But these kids looked like a real team: They followed orders and worked together and were probably friends, which wasn't really like the Science Club either. Jonah didn't have a lot of friends. Actually, he didn't have any. Taking one last look at the group of kids, he hurried after Willona, who was already well past the hallway.

"For the next week, you will be in training," Willona said as he fell into step behind her. "I call the program Space Raider Training 101." She stopped and handed him a sheet of paper. "Here. I've prepared you a syllabus for Day One."

~~SILABUS CYLABUS~~ SYLLABUS?

1. Introduction to the ISR ☺

2. Tour of Sector Three: Refreshments Available

3. Break (Naptime?)

4. Uniform Fitting
5. Bonker Training with Alex—NO ADVENTURING
6. Orientation Session: Ship Schedule
~~7. Rules Pop Quiz~~ (Pretend you didn't see that)
8. Dinner!
9. Bedtime: I DO NOT Tuck In

Jonah frowned as he looked over the syllabus. He had so many questions, it was hard to pick just one. But there was one thing Willona had said that had kind of stood out.

"How do you know the Shrieker preys on Space Raiders?"

Willona just started marching again, and Jonah jogged after her.

"How do you know?" he asked again.

Willona hesitated and looked at him. "Because it's already eaten seven of us."

CHAPTER TWO

SEVEN? JONAH WHISPERED, FEELING HIS knees wobbling again.

She nodded and put her hand on her badge. "May they raid in peace. And that's just on this trip. We are the seventh batch of Space Raiders to travel to the Dark Zone."

"What happened to the first six?"

Willona paused. "We'll find out when we get there." She patted Jonah's shoulder. "It's better not to think of it. Not until you're trained, anyway. Come on. We have a lot to cover."

They walked by an open doorway, and Jonah saw two girls standing beside it, talking quietly. One glanced at him and smiled. She was very pretty, with long, kind of tangled black hair, dark eyes, and tiny dimples on her cheeks.

"Victoria the Avenger," Willona whispered. "Her younger brother, Matt, was one of the seven who were eaten. He was a good kid. I'd just finished training him."

Jonah gave the girl an awkward smile and tried to think. How had he gotten here?

He remembered sitting by himself in his living room. His parents didn't come home from work until eight o'clock, and his older sister, Mara, was at her boyfriend's house. That was nothing new: Jonah was used to being alone. His parents worked until eight o'clock every evening, even on weekends.

And so he was sitting there by himself doing his math homework and eating a ham sandwich with mustard. That was when he'd heard a noise like a window sliding open. Jonah had looked back, frowning. He didn't hear anything else, so he continued with his math homework. He was good at math, but the current problem was a bit tricky.

Then he heard a whisper.

Now Jonah was alarmed. He wasn't an overly brave boy. He was scared of the dark and of forests, and he even hid under the covers during storms until the thunder and lightning stopped. His sister called him a baby. His father said he was "a little weak in the knees." Even his mother said he was more of a thinker than a doer, which he assumed was her motherly way of calling him a coward.

And so he'd stood up and slowly tiptoed into the kitchen, his hands already trembling. He remembered thinking that if his parents had just gotten him a dog like he'd asked for every birthday since he was four years old, this kind of thing wouldn't happen. But his mother said a dog would just ruin their nice white carpets.

Jonah made it to the kitchen and peeked through the window. He froze.

There was a spaceship sitting in his driveway. Someone had come to his house from space. That had to be a bad thing.

"You sure about this?" he heard a man with a deep voice say.

"It says Jonah Hillcrest."

Jonah turned around sharply. The voices were coming from the hallway.

"It just doesn't seem right," the man with the deep voice said.

"We're already way behind schedule. You really want to double-check?"

Jonah crept toward the living room, his whole body shaking. How did they know his name? He needed to get out of here, but they were blocking the front door. The only other way was to get to the back door through the living room. He peeked in. The coast was clear. Summoning his courage, he made a break for the back door.

He was halfway there when he felt a powerful jolt hit him square in the back. His legs suddenly went numb, and he toppled face-first onto the living room floor.

"This better be the right one," the man with the deep voice said.

"I'm sure it is. Oh, he's still awake."

"Not for long. Sleep tight, Jonah. Time to go save the world."

He felt another jolt, and then it suddenly went dark.

When Jonah opened his eyes again, he was here.

He stopped and looked at Willona. "Men kidnapped me," he whispered. "I remember everything now. I tried to run away, but they shot me with something and—"

Willona nodded. "That was the crew. They took all of us."

"I don't understand. Why did no one tell me I was becoming a Space Raider?"

Willona just patted his arm and continued down the hall.

"They don't tell you you're becoming a Space Raider. Once you're selected, they just come for you. It's not a choice to be a hero. It's a job."

Jonah blinked again as Willona marched down the hallway. He tried it three more times and then sighed. She just wasn't going away. Which meant he really was on the *Fantastic Flying Squirrel*. And he really was an Incredible Space Raider.

And he really had left his family behind.

Which of course meant they had sent him here. His mom and dad. They must have known. Maybe his sister, too. She did call him a constant annoyance. But this?

"Coming?" Willona called. "We have a very tight schedule. You're a Space Raider now, which means you have less than a month to get ready to save the universe. But no rush. Just stop and think for a while. Take it all in—"

"All right, I'm coming," Jonah said.

He hurried after her, though he did try one more blink.

Willona led Jonah up and down Squirrel Street for a while longer, pointing out the cafeteria and the bathrooms and even listing the names of the other Space Raiders.

"There's Ben the Brilliant, Kyla the Courageous, Daniel the Ninja—"

"Am I supposed to remember all these names?" Jonah asked.

She glanced at him. "Yes."

Jonah tried to take a better look at Sector Three as they walked. There were a few things he didn't understand. Everything looked old and worn and beaten down: The light panels weren't just flickering, he noticed now—they were covered with dust and grime. The doors were clearly designed to be automatic, but everywhere he looked, Space Raiders were sliding them open by hand. Even the floors were weathered and stained with oil and other dark spots that might just have been blood. Overall, it was a very unpleasant place.

"If we're saving the universe, why don't we have a better ship?" Jonah asked.

Willona looked at him in shock, covering the nearest wall with her hands.

"The *Fantastic Flying Squirrel* is the greatest ship in the fleet," she whispered.

Jonah frowned. "I don't think it can hear you—"

"The *Squirrel* may not look . . . the prettiest," she said slowly, dusting her hands off on her uniform. "But it's the fastest ship in the solar system, and more important, it's very hard to spot. Considering we're sneaking into enemy territory, you're going to appreciate that. It might just save your life. Now say sorry."

"Sorry," Jonah said.

She rolled her eyes. "To the ship, obviously."

"Oh," Jonah murmured. "Sorry . . . *Fantastic Flying Squirrel*."

She smiled. "Better. Now, did you notice the side hallway we walked by?"

"Yeah?"

"Don't go down there, unless you want to be eaten by the Shrieker."

She continued walking, and Jonah hurried after her again. They were heading to the far side of Sector Three now, past the room Jonah had woken up in.

As they walked, Willona explained that the sectors were organized by when the recruits were brought to the ship. The *Squirrel* started at Earth and then stopped at each inhabited planet on the way out of the solar system to grab the new recruits. The Space Raiders from Sector One—which was led by the commander—came entirely from Earth, while Sector Two came from the large colonies on the moon and Mars. Sector Three—Jonah's sector—came from Saturn and Jupiter's moons, and Sector Four came from Pluto and from the moons of Uranus and Neptune. Of course, everyone spoke English anyway—Jonah remembered learning that fifty years ago the Commission for Human Expansion had decided that one official language would be better for human expansion, since people from all over the world would live together in colonies. As a result all humans learned English now, along with their native language.

"But I'm from Earth," Jonah said. "Shouldn't I be in Sector One?"

She smiled. "You should. But you didn't come on with the rest of them. The ship had to go all the way back to Earth for you. Two extra weeks to get one recruit! That's how we knew you were so important. And then the crew brought you to *our* sector in a bag. We don't know why, but obviously you're meant to be here with us."

"The crew brought me in a bag?" Jonah asked incredulously.

Willona nodded and kept walking. "They bring all the recruits in bags. Regular people don't know about the ISR, Jonah. They would panic. This entire program is top secret. No one can see the crew take kids off the street. Those are the rules."

She snapped her fingers. "That reminds me," she said, fishing a piece of paper out of her pocket. "The rules!" She handed it to Jonah. "Try to memorize these."

Jonah frowned and took the paper. It read:

1. NEVER *make contact with Captain White Shark or the crew. Doing so will result in exile, if the crew doesn't kill you first anyway. Which they will.*
2. NEVER *talk about where you came from before joining the* ISR.
3. NEVER *question the commander or a lieutenant.*
4. NEVER *cry or show signs of weakness outside of your quarters.*
5. NEVER *swear or insult other Space Raiders.*
6. NEVER *steal food or water.*
7. NEVER *abandon your post, unless you really have to go to the bathroom.*
8. NEVER, EVER *try to communicate with the Shrieker. It will eat you.*

Jonah frowned. "Why would the crew kill us if we're on an official mission?"

Willona shrugged, considering his question. "Because they're evil. When Earth's first ship went missing, it was full of scientists and soldiers. The best in the solar system. After that, no one would volunteer to go—except Captain White Shark. For some reason, the EETs wouldn't kill him or his crew. I think it's because they only like to destroy things that are good, like us. And because he can survive the trip, Captain White Shark is the only one who can take us. That's why we're stuck with an evil crew that loves to kill Space Raiders."

She narrowed her eyes.

"But when the war is over, we'll come back and take our vengeance. Let's continue."

Willona led him to the end of Sector Three, which Jonah knew because the hall ended at big double doors with black-and-yellow stripes and a handwritten sign saying *sector four*. Willona stopped at the last gray door on the right and pulled it open.

"These are my quarters. Before you start training, I have to give you something."

Jonah followed her into the bedroom. It looked the same as his, except there was a pile of various items in the corner. There was also a photograph sitting on the bed. It was fairly crumpled, but Jonah saw two smiling people holding a little girl with brown hair.

"Who's that?" Jonah asked.

Willona turned around and made a noise like a squeal. She hurried over to the bed and snatched up the photo.

"Nothing," she said quickly. "Left that out. Shouldn't even have it, actually." She tucked the photo under her blanket. "Nothing, though. Never mind that. Classified."

She gave Jonah an awkward smile and headed back to the corner, where she grabbed a pen and a dusty notepad. After a quick check to make sure the pen worked, she handed both to Jonah.

"Your journal."

Jonah looked at the notepad, confused. "I don't need a diary."

She nodded. "Yes you do. Commander's orders. Everyone writes in a journal."

"Why?"

Willona forced another smile. "It helps with the Space Sadness."

"Space Sadness?" Jonah asked, frowning.

"Being on the ship out here . . . sometimes recruits get down. Not me. Not much. Well, sometimes. Writing helps. I know you're used to a tablet, but it's kind of nice to write. Like we're explorers on an old sea ship on Earth."

Jonah didn't want the journal, but he took it anyway and tucked it into his pocket. "Thank you."

She gave him a real smile this time. "It's going to get better. Trust me. You're going to love it here." She patted his arm. "Why don't you take a break? Lie down for a bit. When you get up, you can get your uniform and start training. Jemma will have it finished by now. We need to get you out of that . . . thing."

Jonah looked down. He was still wearing his school uniform: crisp blue pants and a matching jacket with black-and-white trim on the arms and legs. Every student at Pinewood Boys' Academy wore the same outfit. It was a very strict and very expensive private school. Jonah didn't really like it there, but his parents insisted it was good for his future. They always liked to talk about his future.

"What's wrong with this one?"

She made a face. "You almost look like an adult."

"I think that was the point," Jonah said.

"Well, it won't do. You need to dress like a Space Raider." She looked up and away, as if staring at a distant sunrise. "It's not an easy life. But if we don't stand up to the Entirely Evil Things from the Dark Zone, who will?"

Jonah followed her gaze, confused. "About the Entirely Evil Things—"

"I'll take you back now," Willona said, heading for the door. She stopped and glanced back. "Can you not tell anyone about the photo?"

"Yeah, sure," Jonah said.

She smiled. "I'm starting to like you, Jonah. Sure, you look like you're going to faint whenever I mention EETs. And you ask too many questions. And you're not very good with names. But there's something about you. I think you are special. I have no idea what that means, exactly, but it's always good to be special."

"I don't feel very special," Jonah muttered.

"We're all special in the ISR!" Willona said, starting down the hallway. "Billions of kids out there, and we were chosen to save the universe. Why? Who knows! Well, I'm pretty awesome, as you can obviously see, but it's not always so easy to tell. . . ."

Jonah took one last look at the bed, thinking about the photo, and then started after her. As far as he knew, he wasn't awesome at all. If anything, he was kind of a wimp. So why had the *Squirrel* gone all the way back to Earth to get him?

And more important, was it ever going to take him home?

CHAPTER THREE

Dear Mom and Dad,

There's a good chance I'm going to be eaten by the Shrieker or EETs. I was supposed to use this notepad as a diary, but it made more sense to write you a letter. Hopefully it will get to you one day.

I don't think it will make much sense if I explain where I am, so I won't bother. I also hear some people shouting outside, and I'm starting to think something is about to burst into my bedroom soon and eat me. So before that happens, I just wanted to say I love you. I think I was an all right kid, though I probably could have been better. I kept leaving my clothes on the floor. I don't know why. My closet was right there. I was doing my homework when I was abducted, so I guess that's something.

Also, can you please tell Mara I'm sorry I called her the ugliest thing in the universe? While I haven't seen the Shrieker, I'm guessing it's probably uglier. Plus, calling her ugly wasn't very nice in the first place. Maybe tell her I love her too. Not her boyfriend, though. He calls me Jonie when you're not around.

Anyway, I should probably see if I can lock my door or something. I'm hoping I can give you this letter myself. If not, good-bye.

Sincerely,
Jonah

Jonah read his letter over a few times and then tucked the journal safely under his blanket, satisfied. His parents always said you should speak formally in letters, and he'd tried his best. Even the penmanship was fairly good, considering he hadn't written anything with a pen since he was seven, and even then they just did it in history class to see how people used to write. You could barely even tell his hands were trembling when he wrote it.

He looked around the small bedroom and noticed something on the wall beside the door. He got up and hurried over. It was writing. It was hard to read on the dark-metal walls, but when he got really close he could make out five different names written there.

ROBERT THE GREAT WAS HERE. GO, ISR!

Imran the Intelligent stayed in this room

ADAM THE TITAN LIVED HERE. I'M COMING FOR YOU, EETs

Danielle the Dynamo was here. Best Space Raider Ever

HOME OF SHOEN THE SLICK. ON THE WAY TO HELP THE FIRST RECRUITS!

Jonah decided to add his name to the list. There wasn't much else to do.

He was just turning away to grab his pen when he noticed more writing in the corner, away from the others. It was faded and even harder to read. Peering really close, Jonah managed to make it out:

I want to go home.

Niraj

Jonah frowned. That one didn't quite match the others.

There was a knock. Jonah hesitated and then decided the Shrieker probably wouldn't knock first. He slowly answered the door.

It was Willona.

"Get some sleep?" she asked brightly.

Jonah shook his head. "Not really. Just stared out the window for a while."

He didn't want to admit he was already using the journal.

"Beautiful, isn't it?"

Jonah turned back to the window. The endless blackness of space was rolling by, spotted with little twinkling stars. "Kind of scary, actually," he said.

"Yeah, I'm glad I don't have one," she agreed. She glanced at him. "Sorry. Now we have things to do. First up, you need a uniform." Willona pulled a little silver-wrapped bar out of her pocket. "Here. I brought you a food bar. You must be hungry."

"Yeah, actually," Jonah said, accepting the bar gratefully. "Thanks."

"There's a rumor going around about us," Willona said, leading Jonah down Squirrel Street. "I said you had nice eyes, and now everyone thinks we're dating." She looked back and laughed. "Like I have time for a boyfriend. I have a career to worry about."

Jonah just frowned and followed her. She really was a strange girl. They headed down the hallway toward Sector Two, and once again there were Space Raiders marching around. A small group was gathered outside one doorway, talking in hushed voices.

"What was all the shouting about?" Jonah asked.

"One of the guards heard shrieking down the Haunted Passage. Whenever that happens, we all clear the hallway in case the Shrieker attacks. Can't be too careful."

"Oh," Jonah murmured. He was sorry he'd asked.

He peeled off the silver wrapper as they walked and

took a bite. He almost spit it out. It was dry and crumbly and tasted like kidney beans.

Willona smiled. "We also call them bean bars. But it's all we have, so you better get used to them."

She stopped in front of a door and knocked. "Jemma?"

A girl pulled the door open and grinned. Her straw-colored hair perched like a bird's nest on her head, bright blue eyes, and freckles dotted her nose and cheeks. Jonah also noticed a few blistered burn marks on her hands, though it was hard to get a good look at them because her hands were always moving.

"Nice to meet you, Jonah," she said, giving him a quick hug that took Jonah completely by surprise. He glanced at Willona.

"She's a hugger," Willona said simply.

Jemma shrugged. "Too much saluting on this ship. Come in. It's ready."

She quickly fetched his uniform from a pile on the floor. He saw another pile of badges that she was sewing with an old kit like one his grandma used to have in her attic.

"Not quite as nice as that one," she said ruefully, looking at Jonah's school uniform. "But rules are rules."

Willona and Jemma stepped out to let him change, and he reluctantly took off his blue uniform and slid into the coarse brown fabric. The uniform was a one-piece jumper that zipped up the front, with two deep pockets and a black belt to keep it snug at the waist. It hung a bit loosely from his arms, but he could tell that Jemma had tried to stitch it to fit his skinny body. The pant legs had been hemmed, as had the sleeves. He ran his fingers over the ISR badge on the chest, which was an inverted black triangle with the red letters in the middle.

"You can come in," he said.

Willona and Jemma hurried back inside.

"Not bad, not bad," Jemma mused, looking him up and down. "A little baggy."

"He'll grow into it," Willona said.

Jemma smiled and scooped up the blue uniform. Her teeth were a bit yellow and crooked, but it was somehow comforting when she smiled. It seemed like she meant it.

"He looks like a Space Raider," Jemma said. She looked down at Jonah's socked feet. "Keep your shoes, Jonah. I'll turn the rest of the uniform into a blanket."

Jonah slid on his polished black shoes. "Can I at least have the blanket?"

Jemma laughed. "Sure. Good luck with your training."

She bundled up his old uniform, and Jonah noticed that her sleeves had rolled back just a little. The burn marks continued all the way up her arms. He returned her smile and followed Willona down the hallway.

They soon stopped in front of another door, and Willona knocked again.

"What are we doing now?" Jonah asked.

"*You* are starting training with Alex," Willona said, leaving Jonah at the door and continuing down Squirrel Street. "We have another lesson in an hour. And try to memorize those rules. There will be a test!" She paused. "I mean there could be. It's a pop quiz . . . so who knows? Maybe there won't be. But study. I would definitely study."

Jonah stood by the doorway as the small, shrewd-looking boy known as Alex the Adventurer laid a hand-drawn map out on the floor. There were six metal pipes leaning against the wall in his bedroom, which looked exactly like Jonah's, minus the window.

Finally, when the map was laid out and held down by four pipes, Alex glanced up. He looked like a very clever mouse. His sandy hair was wispy and a bit long, hanging down beside his big round ears. His eyes were blue and moved around a lot, as if he wanted to see everything all the time. In short, he looked like the perfect adventurer.

"Jonah, right?" His voice was squeaky. Jonah wasn't surprised.

Jonah nodded. "Yeah."

"Sit down."

Jonah sat down cross-legged in front of the map. Its lines were a bit wobbly, and apparently drawn with an old black pen.

"This is the *Fantastic Flying Squirrel*," Alex said, using a metal pipe as a pointer. "As you can see, there are many different parts. Some I've seen, but some of this information has been passed down from the second and first most important adventurers."

Jonah looked up. "You're the third most important?"

Alex swelled with pride. "Recently promoted from fourth."

"Congratulations," Jonah said.

"Thank you," Alex replied curtly, though he seemed pleased that Jonah had said something. His ears even turned red. "As I was saying, there are many different parts of the *Squirrel*. I'm sure Willona told you about the sectors. But more important are these two." He pointed at a long section at the top of the ship and a rectangular section near the back. "You are not to go in these two areas. Ever. Period. Never. If you go there, you won't come back. Trust me."

"What are they?" Jonah asked quietly.

"The top section is the bridge and the quarters. That's where Captain White Shark and his crew live. Nasty bunch. If you run into them, you're a goner."

Jonah nodded. "And the back?"

"The Unknown Zone. Home of the Shrieker," Alex said quietly, glancing at the door. "If you hear shrieking, run and hide. It comes fast. And it takes Space Raiders, too."

"Willona said you've already lost seven."

Alex solemnly put his hand on his patch. "May they raid in peace."

"What does that mean?" Jonah whispered.

"I don't know," Alex said. "But it seems like a nice thing to say."

Jonah pointed at the rest of the sections on the ship. "What are all these areas?"

"The Wild Zones. No one has a claim there. Only the bravest ever enter those areas. Except this one," he said, pointing at a hallway that ran alongside Squirrel Street. "The Haunted Passage. I go there all the time."

"Why?"

He shrugged. "Because I'm an adventurer. Actually, I'm due for a scouting mission again. Might be good training. Want to check it out?"

"Not really," Jonah said.

"Don't worry—it's safe. I've gone there four times and never seen the Shrieker." He stood up and handed Jonah a metal pipe. "Here, take a bonker. You'll get your own when you're trained, but you can borrow this one for now."

"A bonker?" Jonah asked, taking the pipe.

He pretended to hit something. "You know, like, *bonk*. It's the sound it makes when it hits someone. We think. Never actually hit anyone yet. Now let's get going. It'll be good for you. Get used to the ship a little."

"I guess," Jonah said. He really didn't like the sound of that Shrieker.

"That's the spirit," Alex said, starting for the door. "You'll fit in just fine."

Five minutes later, Jonah and Alex were walking down a very dark corridor. Jonah could see why it was called the Haunted Passage. Only a few light panels worked here, and even those flickered like candles. Every footstep sounded incredibly loud in the still, heavy silence. The only thing Jonah heard was the ship's engine, which sounded like a moaning ghost in the darkness. He was already trembling.

"Cool, right?" Alex whispered.

"Supercool," Jonah said.

He didn't want to seem like a wimp. But he'd seen

the way the hall guards looked at him when he walked by. Like Jonah was a goner.

"Where does it go?" he asked quietly.

"It leads to the Unknown Zone." He glanced at Jonah. "You ever go on any adventures at home?"

"Not really," Jonah said. "I went into a forest once."

"I forgot you used to be from Earth! You're the last recruit. The special one."

"I guess," Jonah said. "Where are you from?"

Alex looked away. "I *used* to be from a colony on Pluto. But that's in the past. Ancient history. Not to be spoken of. Now I'm from space. So are you, by the way."

"Right," Jonah said. "Do you know where this ship is going—"

He was cut off by a chilling, cackling laugh echoing down the hallway. It bounced around in the silence, growing louder and louder as it ran past Jonah's ears.

He looked at Alex, who had gone completely white.

"It's here," Alex whispered.

CHAPTER FOUR

THE LAUGHTER GREW LOUDER, ACCOMPANIED by bone-chilling shrieks.

"We're stuck out in the open!" Alex said, looking panicked.

"There!" Jonah said, pointing at a small air grate. "Get in!"

The two boys hurried to the air grate, and Alex pulled it open. They crawled inside the duct, and Alex quickly pulled the grate shut behind them. They just made it.

Before Alex could even let go of the grate, the Shrieker arrived. It ran by in a flash, its feet slapping off the cold metal. Jonah tried to get a look, but he could only see the silhouettes of legs through the grate. He heard it, though: growls and howls and loud, inhuman laughter. His skin went cold as it ran by, and only when the voice was small in the distance did Alex finally turn to Jonah, his face mostly hidden by the deep shadows in the air duct.

"That was a close one," Alex whispered.

Jonah could barely bring himself to speak. His hands were trembling.

"What do we do now?" he whispered.

Alex turned back to the grate. "We wait. If we don't hear anything for ten minutes, we'll head back to Squirrel Street."

"The seven who were eaten . . . were they all adventurers?"

Alex looked at him. "How do you think I got promoted?"

After waiting for what seemed like a very long ten minutes, Jonah and Alex climbed out of the grate. Jonah looked down at his uniform. It was covered in dust.

"Did you know that dust is mostly made out of dead human skin cells?" Alex said brightly, though he was still peering down the hallway.

Jonah grimaced. "No."

"Yep," Alex said, starting back down the Haunted Passage. "There's also dead dust mites in there." He brushed some dust off his arms. "Pretty neat, right?"

"I guess," Jonah replied. He was listening intently for the shouting voice. Whatever that thing was, he really didn't want to run into it again.

"You know, you really saved my keister back there," Alex said.

"Your what?" Jonah asked.

"Keister," Alex said. "It's part of the ship code. No swearing."

Jonah frowned and glanced at him. "What is a keister?"

Alex looked behind them and then pointed at his rear. "You know: tush. Heinie. Bumper rumper."

"You mean your—"

"Yes," Alex said quickly. "Don't say it. You could end up in the brig."

"You have a brig?"

Alex nodded. "Yep. Martin the Marvelous is in there right now. He took a food bar without asking. Not good. He got a three-day sentence from the lieutenant." He smiled. "But enough of that unpleasant stuff. The fact of the matter is, you just saved my caboose. That was some quick thinking. You need a name. A good one."

They walked past a metallic blue door covered in rust spots. Jonah had been too busy staring down the hallway to notice the door last time, but now he took a good look at it. There was no handle. A smashed control panel was mounted next to it on the wall, and red and green wires still dangled below it. But of greater concern to Jonah were the deep scratches running all across the door. They looked like they had been made by something with very powerful claws.

"What is—"

"Classified," Alex said. "Now, your name. It has to be something impressive."

"I don't know," Jonah said, still looking back nervously at the door.

"It's easy! Just add a cool word to make a title."

"Why do we do that again?" Jonah asked.

"Because if we had normal names, people wouldn't know how incredible we are," Alex said.

"Oh," Jonah said. The more questions he asked, the more confused he was.

They finally made it back to Squirrel Street and passed by the two grim-faced hall guards. They gave Alex a curt nod and looked at Jonah like they were surprised he had returned.

Alex leaned in close to one. "We ran into the Shrieker. Keep an eye out."

They both straightened immediately.

"How about Jonah the Incredible?" Alex suggested as they continued walking. "Surprisingly, that's not used very much. Too obvious, maybe."

Jonah frowned. "I don't think I've ever been called incredible."

Alex smiled. "Well, you have now." He paused. "Jonah the Now Incredible."

Jonah just glanced at him and shook his head. He didn't want a name. Even an impressive one like that. He wanted to get off this ship of strange soldier children and shrieking monsters that may or may not have razor-sharp claws. He wanted to go home.

He was about to tell Alex just that when Willona turned the corner, flung her hands out in exasperation, and hurried toward them.

"Where have you two been?" she asked sharply. "I had an orientation session planned for twenty minutes ago."

"We went adventuring," Alex said sheepishly.

"Shocking," Willona replied, glaring at him. "Come on, Jonah."

"We saw the Shrieker," Alex said.

Willona looked at him in disbelief. "You *saw* it?"

"Well, not really," he said. "But it was real close."

"You better go file a report. The lieutenant will want to hear all about it."

She grabbed Jonah's arm and carted him down the hallway.

"I mean, really," she said, shaking her head. "You're disrupting my schedule, Jonah."

"Jonah the Now Incredible," Alex corrected, hurrying along behind them.

Willona glanced at him, then at Jonah. "That's pretty good."

She continued to pull Jonah along, and he looked back at Alex for support. Alex just grinned and flipped him a thumbs-up.

"Told you," he mouthed.

Jonah collapsed onto his cot. After another hour-long

lesson with Willona covering everything from food schedules to emergency drills—including Shrieker attacks, hull breaches, and how to deal with a crying Space Raider—he was exhausted. There was a lot to cover. Of course, the response to most emergencies was to run away, other than the crying Space Raider one. For that you were to remind the individual that crying was against the rules and then report the kid to the lieutenant.

There was also a test on the rules, which he'd failed. Willona had just shaken her head and ordered him to take a nap before dinner.

In his room, Jonah looked at his pillow. The white pillowcase was yellowed with age, and he didn't even want to guess at the last time it was washed. He felt something sticking into his back and remembered that he'd put the journal under his blanket. He pulled it out and rolled onto his stomach. Taking out the pen, he turned to the second page.

Dear Mom and Dad,

I know I already wrote you a letter, but I figured I might as well write another one. It does seem to help with the loneliness.

I know I said I love you already, but I forgot to mention Grandma and Grandpa. Can you tell them I love them, too? Also, sorry that I broke Grandma's vase two years ago. By the way, that was me, not the cat. I guess also say sorry to Charles too. Is he still alive? He was pretty old.

I feel like things are just happening all around me, and I can't seem to keep up. I miss you guys. I miss my own room and my own bed. I miss ham sandwiches. These bean bars are disgusting. I keep wondering if I'll ever get home.

Anyway, I'm pretty tired. I think I have bonker training when I wake up, so I should have a nap. Bonkers are weapons, by the way. I love you. And Mara. Still not her boyfriend. Have they broken up yet? I guess it doesn't matter. But I hope so.

If this is my last letter, good-bye.

Sincerely,
Jonah

Jonah read it over and decided it was another excellent letter. Closing the journal, he rolled onto his back again, said a silent good night to his parents, and fell asleep.

• • •

He woke to knocking. Blinking sleepily, Jonah rubbed his eyes and went to get the door.

"Have a nice nap?" Willona asked.

He rubbed his eyes again. "Time to train again already?"

Willona shook her head. "Not quite. It's dinnertime."

She led him down the hallway, and Jonah just kept blinking sleepily. He really could have used a few more hours of sleep. Willona took him to the cafeteria, then turned to him and smiled.

"Welcome to the ISR."

She slid the door open, and Jonah's eyes widened. The cafeteria was packed with Space Raiders, and they all cheered and clapped as soon as Willona and Jonah stepped through the door. He saw Jemma and Alex and even the girl with the tangled black hair and dimples.

"What's this all about?" Jonah asked, looking around in amazement.

The cafeteria didn't look like the one at Pinewood Academy. It was about five times the size of Jonah's room, and it was made of the same rusted gray metal as the rest of the ship. There were some old stained white cupboards and a sink pressed against one of the walls, as well as four big metal tables to sit at, but Jonah wasn't sure that made it a cafeteria. Large boxes stacked in the corner were labeled RATIONS.

"Alex told the lieutenant about your run-in with the Shrieker and how your quick thinking saved his life," Willona said, grinning from ear to ear. "He's decided to give you a Badge of Bravery. On your first day! It's unheard of. So we're having a little celebration. Go on."

Jonah rubbed his eyes again and walked into the cafeteria, where Alex greeted him with a big smile and a salute. The other Space Raiders slapped him on the back and shook his hand, including the girl with dimples. Jonah felt himself blushing. No one outside of his parents had ever congratulated him before. Once, one of his teachers said "good work" when he won a school science fair, but that wasn't really the same thing.

A tall boy with dark skin and a shaved head walked up to Jonah and saluted. He looked about fourteen, but he walked and saluted like a real soldier.

"This is Lieutenant Gordon," Willona said. "Leader of Sector Three."

The lieutenant shook Jonah's hand. "Congratulations, Jonah the Now Incredible. You're clearly going to make a great Space Raider. Jemma will sew your Badge of Bravery on first thing tomorrow. You should be very proud. How about another cheer?"

The assembled Space Raiders cheered, and Jonah just smiled stupidly and let himself be led to a seat at one of the tables. They ate disgusting bean bars and drank stale water from the tap, but it was one of the best dinners of Jonah's life.

The Space Raiders smiled and talked to him and

treated him like he was part of the family. Alex told the story of their trip to the Haunted Passage over and over again, and each time it got more and more dangerous and exciting. No one seemed to mind.

By the end, Jonah was basically staring the Shrieker in the eye and fending off its terrible claws as he pushed Alex into the grate and dove in headfirst after him.

The dimpled girl kept glancing over, causing Jonah's cheeks to burn red hot every single time. No girl had ever looked at him on Earth. Well, his sister looked at him all the time, but usually just to tell him to comb his hair.

When everyone was done eating, a boy shouted, "Speech! Speech!"

The shout was taken up by everyone in the room, until Jonah was forced to stand up. He felt his cheeks burning extra hot now. He hated public speaking.

"Uhh . . . ," he started awkwardly. He tried to think back to things his parents had taught him. Ah. Always start by thanking someone. "Thank you, everyone, for the party."

The Spaced Raiders clapped and cheered. So far so good, he thought.

"And, uhh . . . thanks to Alex and Willona for training me so far."

They both beamed. Jonah tried to think of something else to say. He couldn't remember what he was supposed to do after thanking everyone. Should he thank someone else? No. He decided to just go with a little honesty.

"I'm still getting used to all this, I guess. It's kind of weird waking up on an old ship in space with Willona staring down at you. But I'm honored that I was chosen to be a Space Raider. Surprised, maybe, but definitely honored. I guess the only thing I wish is that I could call my parents and tell them I'm all right."

The entire room instantly fell silent. Alex looked like he was about to fall off the bench. Willona put her hand over her mouth. For a few seconds, no one said a word.

"Is something wrong?" Jonah asked.

"Alex, send word to the commander," Lieutenant Gordon said, his dark eyes fixed on Jonah. "Tell her we have a problem."

CHAPTER FIVE

THINGS REALLY CHANGED QUICKLY ON THE *Fantastic Flying Squirrel,* Jonah decided. One second he was the hero of Sector Three, and the next he was being escorted down Squirrel Street like a prisoner. Lieutenant Gordon was walking ahead, while Willona and Alex—who had returned with the summons for a meeting—hurried along behind him.

Twice, an armed guard pulled the big double doors with the black-and-yellow stripes aside to let them pass through each sector. It turned out the other sectors looked the exact same as Sector Three, with flickering light panels and identical gray doors and kids with bonkers marching around in overlarge brown uniforms. The only difference was that there were even more of them. Sector One was packed with Space Raiders.

The lieutenant finally led Jonah to a faded red door in Sector One that was guarded by a tall, very strong-looking girl with vibrant frizzy orange hair tied back in a poof. She stared at Jonah as he approached, her eyes narrowed and probing.

"Erna the Strong," Willona whispered behind him. "Most Important Guard."

Jonah could see why. She was scary.

Erna the Strong pulled the door open, and Jonah nervously walked inside. The room was the biggest one he'd seen so far, and it contained three black metal tables. They were arranged in a U shape, with the open end toward the door. Four Space Raiders were sitting there.

Lieutenant Gordon immediately sat down at one of the side tables, making five. And while two Space Raiders sat at each side table, only one sat at the head table, farthest from the doorway.

Without even asking, Jonah knew it was the commander.

She looked to be about sixteen years old, but her eyes made her seem older. She wore the same plain brown uniform as everyone else, but hers was impeccable. No loose threads. No frayed edges. Her belt looked to be of some fine brown leather. And there was more.

Her long hair was as black as space, but it was streaked with flashes of blue, like bizarre lightning. Her skin was extremely pale, as if it had never seen the sun, and was marked only by a thin white scar that ran from her right cheek to her chin, bridging over her lips. She was pretty, Jonah noted, but not in the nice way. It was the kind of pretty that made him want to run away and hide.

He felt his skin prickling as they all stared at him, and

her worst of all. Even Willona and Alex seemed to shrink away behind him.

"Be super-very polite," Willona whispered.

Erna the Strong closed the door and turned to the front of the room. "Presenting Sara the Splendidly Wise and Brave," she said loudly. Her voice was husky and strong. "Commander of the Incredible Space Raiders from Space."

Jonah just stood there.

"Salute, you nincompoop," Willona said sharply.

Jonah quickly saluted. He'd never done it before, and he hit himself in the nose.

The commander raised a thin black eyebrow. "And you are . . ."

"Jonah the Now Incredible," Willona announced behind him.

"I see. Well, let's get down to business," the commander said. She spoke like someone who was used to giving orders. Every time she looked at Jonah, he felt like she was staring right through him. "You told Lieutenant Gordon you'd like to call your parents. Is that correct?"

"Yes," Jonah said.

A few of the other Space Raiders in the room whispered among themselves.

"When was the last time you saw them?" she asked.

"The morning before I was abducted," Jonah said.

The commander tapped one of her slender fingers on

the table. "And he was the special recruit?" she asked a girl with sandy-blond hair to her right.

The girl nodded.

"First things first," the commander said, her eyes back on Jonah. "Our lives before joining the ISR are all classified. Not to be spoken of. Ever."

Jonah opened his mouth to say something but thought better of it.

"But more important," she continued, "I'm not sure that Jonah the Now Incredible is supposed to be here. And that would be a problem."

Everyone in the room stared at Jonah, frowning.

The commander looked at the girl to her right again. "Samantha the Bravest and Most Daring Adventurer—"

Jonah glanced at Alex, who rolled his eyes.

"I need you to get to the List," the Commander continued. "It won't be easy."

"It never is," Samantha said, shooting Alex just the slightest of smirks.

"Good," the commander said. "We need to see if Jonah is supposed to be here. Until then, Jonah, you may continue your training for hall guard. But you are to be given the lowest priority area: brig-duty. And until I order it, all—*I repeat: all*—information is classified. Especially concerning the Entirely Evil Things from the Dark Zone."

Jonah looked at Willona, who bit her lip and dramatically looked away.

The commander leaned forward, and a lock of that lighting-streaked black hair swept over her face. "If you are the special recruit, I apologize. But we have to be sure."

When Jonah looked around the room, he saw a lot of unfriendly eyes. Even Willona and Alex had taken an almost imperceptible step backward.

"Does this mean I can't call my parents?" Jonah asked.

The commander sat back and sighed.

"I wish I could swear right now," Willona whispered.

Jonah was starting to really dislike the Incredible Space Raiders from Space. First of all, Erna the Strong was currently pushing him down Squirrel Street toward Sector Three's brig. She had her hands on his shoulders, and her fingers were digging in rather uncomfortably. It was official. She was even stronger than she looked.

Second, Willona and Alex, who had so far been his only companions, were walking about twenty feet behind him and doing absolutely nothing to help. They looked a bit upset. Jonah hoped it was because they disapproved of how Erna was treating him.

But worst of all was that he was apparently not even supposed to be here. It wasn't much better, but when Jonah thought he'd been specially chosen for the ISR, that was at least something. Now he was just a possibly accidental passenger who apparently didn't listen to the rules very well and needed to spend a few hours in the brig to consider what he'd done.

They finally reached the brig, and a young boy quickly moved out of the way as Erna the Strong pulled the door open and shoved Jonah inside.

"He stays for three hours," Erna the Strong said gruffly.

The brig guard quickly nodded. He looked petrified.

Before Jonah could say anything else, the door slammed shut, and he was plunged into almost complete darkness. Just a bit of light emanated from one flickering glow panel over the door. Jonah stared at the door for a moment and then turned to find a seat.

"Hello," someone said, and Jonah almost fell backward.

A small boy was standing directly behind him. Jonah couldn't see him very well, except for his very white teeth that caught the light.

"What did you do?" he asked, staring up at Jonah.

"Uhh . . . I mentioned my life before I came here," Jonah said, squinting in the darkness. "Are you Martin the Marvelous, by any chance?"

"Yep. Did they tell you I was bad?" he asked, sounding very concerned.

"No," Jonah said. "Just that you took an extra food bar."

Martin nodded and walked toward the shadowy cot in the corner. "I did. Old habits. I mean . . . I was hungry. Actually, it wasn't even for me. I took it for Whiskerface."

"Who's Whiskerface?"

Martin sat down on the cot, sliding back against the wall and hugging his knees against his chest. He couldn't have been much older than eight or nine.

"The sector rat. Well, he's his own rat. Comes and goes as he pleases. But he seems to like our sector. Probably because I feed him. He's been looking a bit thin."

Jonah sat down beside him. "When did you get here?"

"To the *Squirrel*? Three or four weeks ago, I guess."

"And where did you come from?" Jonah asked.

Martin glanced at him. "I can see why you ended up in the brig. But I guess we're already here, so why not? I came from Ganymede."

"And how did you end up here?"

Martin shrugged. "I went to sleep. Same as always. But when I woke up, I was on the *Squirrel*. Sitting down on the floor. Hurt like a bugger. Willona was standing there, smiling at me and saying welcome to the Incredible Space Raiders. And here I am. Not off to a flying start, I guess. But I'll be good now. I've been in the brig for two days. Not fun in here, let me tell you. Besides, I have to be ready when we hit the Dark Zone.

He leaned in a bit closer.

"Has Alex told you about the scratches on the blue door?"

"I saw them," Jonah whispered.

He nodded. "They say those weren't made by the

Shrieker. They were made by the EETs. The ISR barely fought them off that time. And now we're going back. To fight creatures that can make claw marks in solid steel. So ask yourself: Are you ready? 'Cause we're going to be there in less than a month."

Jonah sat back against the wall, staring into the darkness.

"I really need to get off this ship."

CHAPTER SIX

THREE HOURS IN THE BRIG FELT LIKE THREE DAYS. Jonah spent a lot of time thinking about home, and Martin just sat there with his eyes closed, like he was meditating.

Jonah looked at him. "How come the sectors don't talk to each other?"

Martin's eyes blinked open. "They do once in a while, but only on official business. The commander is in charge of all the Space Raiders, but to make it easier to keep everyone in line, she assigned a lieutenant to take care of the other three sectors. I guess it's easier to control smaller groups."

"Have there been problems before?"

"Not that I know of," Martin said. "Besides me. Well, a few adventurers broke the rules and went traveling through the ship without permission. But they were eaten."

"How do you know?"

He shrugged. "They never came back."

Jonah looked at the door, thinking about the ship. It

was all so strange. He still had so many questions. Who had sent them here? How were they supposed to kill EETs with metal pipes?

But there was one question in particular he needed to ask. The one he'd been thinking about ever since he'd gotten here.

"Has anyone tried to go home?" he asked quietly.

Martin laughed. "Of course not."

"Why?"

Martin looked at him, his eyes catching the faint light from the glow panel.

"Because we are home."

Jonah was just about to ask another question when the door finally slid open again. Jonah shielded his face from the light and stood up, eager to be out of the small, stuffy room.

Willona stood there, looking sympathetic. "How was it?"

"Dark," Jonah said. He glanced at Martin. "Can he come?"

"He has one more day," Willona said. "Lieutenant's orders."

"It's all right," Martin said stoically. "Do the crime, pay the time."

Jonah nodded, then followed Willona out into the hallway. With a screech, the door was slammed shut again. He caught one last glimpse of poor Martin before it closed.

"Three days in there is a long time," Jonah said.

"Food preservation is important," Willona replied. "Though I do like Whiskerface." She started marching down the hallway. "Now that your imprisonment is over, we can get back to training. Well, limited training. Sorry. But brig duty is honorable. You can't let the convicts escape."

"You mean Martin?" Jonah asked.

Willona paused. "Yes."

A group of Space Raiders walked past, and Jonah noticed that not one of them smiled or saluted at him. In fact, they all pointedly looked away and stopped talking.

"What was that all about?" Jonah asked.

Willona hesitated. "They don't think you belong here."

"I gathered that," Jonah said. "But why? Why is everyone acting so weird whenever I mention my parents?"

Willona glanced back at him. "We're all orphans, Jonah. Every single Space Raider on this ship."

Jonah stopped. "What?"

She just kept marching, and Jonah had to jog to catch up. "Every one of us," she said, her voice a little strange, "even me. Did you think they were going to pick kids with families to fly across the galaxy and risk their lives? They needed kids, and we were the best choice. Not just that, of course. We were picked for a special reason. Space Raiders have already learned to fend for ourselves and face adversity and conquer fear. We were picked from hundreds of thousands of orphans because we're the best of all. Except you." She paused. "You have parents. And that's why they think you're a mistake."

Jonah just hurried along behind her, trying to take it all in. It made a lot more sense now. But if that was true, then why had they taken him?

Willona smiled. "Don't worry about it. I'm sure you belong here. You must be extra brave if they picked you. You're already saving lives, remember? You're a hero."

"Thanks," Jonah said. "But I hope I don't belong here."

Willona glanced back at him, forced a smile, and kept walking. "I'll just pretend I didn't hear that. You were in the brig. I can see how that might make you unhappy. I haven't been, though if you keep making me look bad, I'm sure they'll move my cot in there."

She led him to her room, which they'd been using for lessons. He sat down on the bed as usual and watched as she scooped up her notepad, adjusted her glasses, and found where they'd left off.

"How come you're not avoiding me like everyone else?" Jonah asked.

She looked up. "Because we have work to do." She returned to her notes. "The history of the ISR; Lesson Number One: The First Mission."

"Is there going to be another test?"

She looked up again. "Of course. And try to remember to raise your hand."

Willona kept reading. "'Three years ago, the Commission for Human Expansion, or CHE, created the Space Raider program following the discovery of the EETs.'"

Jonah frowned. His parents often discussed the commission. The CHE was a well-known government branch created at the beginning of the space-colonization age. It was rumored to be involved in a lot of questionable practices, including environmental destruction on new planets, forced migrations, and strict new laws. The CHE was led by a man named Daren Elling, a shadowy figure. Jonah remembered his mom saying the entire commission should be shut down, and Elling thrown in prison.

"'The first batch of Space Raiders was recruited from across the solar system. Only the best and brightest were chosen. The commander had already been chosen ahead of time, and she welcomed the new recruits to the ship and informed them of their noble task. They received uniforms and bonkers, since normal weapons don't work in the energy void of the Dark Zone. And while some were afraid, they bravely accepted their mission, and they still fight on against the EETs. For no Space Raider will abandon their mission until the EETs are gone and the universe is safe from evil.' Any questions?"

"Who wrote that story?"

Willona paused. "The commander, I assume. I copied it off a sheet Lieutenant Gordon gave me."

"Were they all orphans too?"

"Yes," Willona said. "We cover that in the next section; The Makings of a Great Space Raider: Courage, Intelligence, Teamwork, and a Hard Life to Make You Strong."

"Which I didn't have."

"No," she agreed. "But maybe you have other qualities. You'll just have to figure out what those are."

As she read on about the second mission of the ISR, Jonah thought about what Willona had said. But no matter how hard he tried, he couldn't think of anything that would make him a great Space Raider. He should have known better.

Jonah Hillcrest could never be a hero.

An hour later, Alex the Adventurer stood facing Jonah with a bonker in his hand. They were standing in the side hallway that ran off of Squirrel Street, and the two guards were sneaking glances at them, though they quickly looked away whenever Jonah noticed.

Alex was treating Jonah a little more formally than before, though he still snuck him a little smile when he handed Jonah his own bonker.

"As you know, Sector Three has one main hallway," Alex said. "Squirrel Street. All the bedrooms, the bathroom facilities, and the cafeteria are there." He gestured around them. "But there is another hallway that intersects Squirrel Street in our sector and leads to the Haunted Passage. Each sector has one of these hallways. We don't go down those. Well, you and I did, and you saw what happened. Each of those hallways is guarded. This one is called Death Alley."

Jonah looked around in alarm.

"Don't worry," Alex said. "The other three are called Last Chance Lane, Terror Drive, and No Escape Avenue. Kind of a theme." He pointed at the two guards with his bonker. "So that's two guards on duty in Death Alley, and two at each double door. And one at the brig. Which is where you come in."

"Yay," Jonah said.

"Not the most exciting," Alex agreed, "but at least you're not in Death Alley. No offense," he said to the two guards, who nodded.

"So I just stand in front of a door with this bonker?" Jonah asked.

"Well, there's a bit more to it than that," Alex said. "Sure, you're guarding the brig for the trip, but you have to be ready to fight when we get to the Dark Zone. There are no guards and adventurers and greeters when we get there. Just Space Raiders."

Jonah looked at the bonker. "Don't I just hit things with it?"

Alex sighed. "No. There is an art to this. Watch."

Alex stepped back and suddenly jabbed the bonker outward with a thrust. He quickly swiped an imaginary weapon aside, took a big swing with two hands, and then did a spin onto the floor, attacking someone's imaginary legs.

"Impressive," Jonah said.

"I'm not the third most important adventurer for nothing," Alex said proudly, getting to his feet. "I'm also a weapons master. I was going to put it in my name, but I thought it would be too long. I still could, I guess. I have to talk to Lieutenant Gordon."

"Who was that other girl with the commander?" Jonah asked. "Samantha the Bravest and Most Daring Adventurer—"

"That would be my sister," Alex said sourly. "She would be back here with us, but she made one little trip to the List and now—"

"What's the List?" Jonah asked.

Alex glanced at the guards and lowered his voice. "It's a manifest. It has the names of all the Space Raiders on this mission. My sister went adventuring the first day we were here and found it on the third level. It was just sitting on the floor in the middle of the hall—one of the crew members must have dropped it. The commander told her to leave it there in case the crew came back for it, but she was so impressed, she gave my sister a promotion to first most important adventurer." He made a face. "It was just luck. Anyway, let's get back to—"

Suddenly, he was interrupted by shouting. This time it wasn't coming from deep in the Wild Zones. It was coming from Sector Three.

"What the . . . ," Alex said.

Space Raiders began running past Death Alley, heading farther up Squirrel Street. Willona suddenly burst around the corner, looking panicked.

"Jonah, get back to your quarters," she said.

"What is—," Jonah started.

"Now," she said sharply. "Alex, they need you."

Alex nodded, then hurried down the hallway. "Take him back," he said to Willona.

She grabbed Jonah's arm and pulled him toward his bedroom. He looked back down Squirrel Street and saw a group of Space Raiders forming outside Lieutenant Gordon's quarters. The lieutenant was in the hallway, shouting orders.

"What's going on?" Jonah asked.

Willona didn't answer. She just pulled him all the way to his bedroom and pushed him inside. She grabbed the door, about to slam it shut, but Jonah stopped it.

"Tell me," he said.

Willona glanced down the hallway and then leaned in. "Two guards are missing," she said quietly. "From our sector. Gone without a trace."

She tried to close it again, but Jonah stopped her.

"Is that what happened to the other kids?"

"No," she said. "The other seven all disappeared in the Wild Zones. Never from the sectors." She met his eyes. "Don't you understand? The boundaries are broken. It's war."

Jonah stepped backward, and Willona slammed the door shut.

CHAPTER SEVEN

Dear Mom and Dad,

Things just keep getting worse. Now it turns out I might not even belong here, which is fine, except we're already in the middle of space, and I can't exactly leave. Of course, they also told me this right after I got my new name: Jonah the Now Incredible. I know it's a bit strange, but I kind of liked it. It sounds impressive.

I've never really done much that's impressive. I mean, I won three science fairs, but you only got to see one, and you kind of missed my demonstration. I know Dad wanted me to play sports like him and Mara. I just wasn't very good at it.

I wish I knew why everyone doesn't like me. I mean, I didn't want to come here. I want to do my math homework and go to school. I know that sounds weird, but I liked doing my math homework. Homework here is all about things that are probably going to eat me in three weeks. It really makes you miss math.

People didn't like me much on Earth, either. They picked on me at school. . . . I know I told you about it sometimes, but it was pretty much every day. Peter was the worst. He called me Big Ears and pushed me around and told me I didn't belong at Pinewood. He might have been right. I never told you this, but I didn't really like Pinewood. It was all rich kids who were kind of stuck up and definitely mean.

Anyway, everyone is shouting again, and I think the monster really might come and eat me this time. I wish I'd had more bonker training. I never even learned how to do that spin. It looked really cool.

If this is my last letter, good-bye.

Sincerely,
Jonah

Jonah put the journal under his blanket and lay there for a while, listening to the shouting voices and running feet. He really wanted to see what was happening, but he also didn't want to be eaten by the Shrieker, so he just stayed put.

After another twenty minutes or so of shouting, there was a knock at the door. Jonah quickly hurried over and opened it.

"Hey," Willona said, glancing down the hallway. She looked a bit nervous.

"What's going on?" he asked quickly.

"The commander is here," she said. "With Erna the Strong. They've collected everyone in front of Lieutenant Gordon's quarters. For a memorial service."

Jonah frowned. "The guards have only been gone for an hour."

"I know, but we like to remember the missing before we make plans," she said. "It's the nice thing to do. And we have to make plans. Someone has violated the treaty."

"We have a treaty?" Jonah asked.

"Not technically," Willona said.

Jonah stepped into the hallway. "Well, shouldn't we get to the service—"

Willona stopped him. "A few of the others . . . don't think you should be there. But I argued and said you should. That everyone from Sector Three should be there. So just don't pay any attention to them. You're a Space Raider. You have a uniform and a bonker. What more can you ask?" She smiled. "Let's go."

Jonah followed her down Squirrel Street and saw that

the entire sector was gathered in the hallway, minus two guards and Martin the Marvelous. Even from there, he could see the commander and Erna the Strong towering over the others. He made a mental note not to break any rules. He really didn't want to go back to the brig.

When Jonah and Willona reached the edge of the group, the commander's cold green eyes flicked to Jonah. He half expected her to tell him to leave, but she just turned back to the others.

"We meet here today in honor of Kyla the Courageous and Daniel the Ninja." She glanced at Lieutenant Gordon. "Is that right?"

He nodded somberly.

"Today these two brave hall guards were taken from Death Alley. They were doing their duty to the ISR, and so we will remember them as heroes. We hope to find them one day with all our lost recruits, but if we don't, we won't forget them."

The commander put her hand on her badge.

"May they raid in peace."

"May they raid in peace," the Space Raiders repeated.

Jonah watched as the kids all lowered their hands again and noticed that many of them shot him suspicious and unfriendly glares. One in particular—the tall, wiry boy with short black hair and dark eyes that he'd seen leading a bonker training session—was really staring, his lips curled in a sneer.

Jonah made a mental note to stay away from him.

"Now," the commander said, "You all have questions. So do I. We don't know if this was Captain White Shark and his crew or the Shrieker. Until we know, we can't do anything rash. If we step over the wrong boundary, we'll have two enemies to fight."

One young girl put up her hand, and the commander nodded at her.

"Kyla the Courageous was my friend," the girl said. "We have to do something."

There was a murmur of approval in the crowd. Erna the Strong watched them closely.

"I agree," the commander said. "But we must act wisely. I will send out two adventurers to try to gather information. Alex the Adventurer and the second most important adventurer will go."

Everyone looked at Alex, who smiled proudly.

"One will try to find out more about the Shrieker, and the other, Captain White Shark. When they have their information, we can make a decision."

"What about Samantha the Bravest and Most Daring Adventurer?" one boy asked, before quickly putting up his hand, looking terrified that he'd broken a rule.

Erna the Strong looked at the commander, but she shook her head.

"I know these are difficult times," the commander said, looking over the crowd. "I can forgive a mistake.

But in times like these, the rules are more important than ever. We have to stay calm." She turned to the boy. "Samantha is on another mission right now. She is currently traveling to the List to learn more about our newest recruit."

The entire gathering of Space Raiders looked at Jonah, who smiled uncomfortably. Willona took a quick step away from him.

"How convenient," the mean-looking boy with black hair muttered.

A few more comments filtered through the group.

"Enough," the commander said. "Jonah is a Space Raider until proven otherwise. Just on limited brig duty and with no right to any answers about anything."

Jonah could tell by the looks on everyone's faces that nobody considered him a Space Raider. Maybe Jemma, Alex, and Willona, though Willona had already taken another step away from him. Jonah wanted to tell them that he didn't care if he was a Space Raider and that he just wanted to go home, but one threatening glance from Erna the Strong convinced him otherwise. He remembered those iron-strong hands.

So Jonah just looked down at the floor and pretended he didn't feel them staring.

"Our adventurers will set out in an hour," the commander said, "once they've had a chance to prepare and say their good-byes." She paused. "Just in case."

Alex wasn't looking as proud anymore.

"When they return, we'll meet again. And until then, make sure you check on the guards every hour. We don't want to lose anyone else."

With that, the commander nodded at Erna the Strong, and the two girls headed back down Squirrel Street toward Sector Two. Everyone watched them go, their footsteps echoing down the silent corridor.

Finally, Lieutenant Gordon turned to the group. "You heard the commander. Back to your stations."

Reluctantly, the assembled Space Raider started breaking off. As they did, many gave parting glares to Jonah. Some even whispered a few last comments, including, "You're no Space Raider," "Spy," and probably the worst, since it was exactly what Jonah wanted to do, "Go home."

But even if that's what he wanted, it still hurt. It hurt when Alex left without looking at him. It hurt when the girl with dimples looked at him like he was the Shrieker. And it hurt when Willona waited until everyone had left before she came over.

She gave him a reassuring pat on the arm. "Things will get better," she said, though she kept her voice down. "When Samantha finds out you're on the List, they'll all say sorry. Well, not the commander. Or Erna the Strong. Or Lieutenant Gordon. But the regular kids. Even Ben the Brilliant." She grimaced. "I hate calling him that."

"Is that the boy with the black hair?" Jonah asked.

"Yep. He's not very nice. I'm not even sure if he's that smart, now that I think about it." Willona shrugged. "Rules are rules. He's probably not sure I'm that awesome, even though it should be pretty obvious. Are you hungry?"

Jonah frowned. "I thought I had to go back to training?"

"Well, Alex is going to be busy preparing," Willona said. "He needs to study his maps. Might as well take a break. I'd train you, but I'm not a very good fighter. That's why I'm the official greeter, I guess. Come on. Let's get you a food bar."

They started down Squirrel Street. Willona was really marching now, swinging her arms and raising her knees with exaggerated precision. Jonah supposed she was trying to set a calming example for the others. He just walked along behind her.

"Why did you mention Ben the Brilliant?" Jonah asked. "You said even him. How come?"

Willona glanced back. "Because he wants to exile you."

"What?" Jonah said.

Willona stopped. "Yeah. He was asking people to vote." She waved a hand in dismissal. "Don't worry. If you're on the List, they can't exile you."

"And if I'm not?" Jonah asked.

She forced a smile and kept marching. "Then they voted to exile you. Twenty-eight to three."

Jonah accepted a food bar from the official food sorter, a very serious-looking girl named Lyana the Forgotten. Jonah had wanted to ask her why she'd chosen that as a name, but she was clearly one of the twenty-eight kids who had voted to exile him. She'd looked very sour when Willona asked for the food bar, and only when Willona had stood there with her hands on her hips and reminded Lyana of the commander's words had she finally fetched him one.

"You don't get another one until tomorrow," Lyana said coolly.

She had long black hair that was braided down her back and interwoven with a few blue ribbons. Her eyes were big and brown, but they looked very sad or very angry. Jonah would have felt bad for her if she didn't keep looking like she wanted to hit him over the head with a box.

"What about dinner?" Willona asked.

"He missed lunch. So this counts as dinner. He can come get breakfast in the morning. If Samantha doesn't come back by then." She glanced at Jonah. "After that we don't need to worry about it."

"I like your ribbons," Jonah said.

It was a bit of a long shot, but his mother had once

told him that if someone didn't like you, you should say something nice about them. He thought back to that day.

"Jonah?" his mother had said, sitting down on the bed beside him.

She was always dressed very nicely. She worked in an office, and so every day she wore crisp gray suits with shiny black shoes, and her hair was neatly combed. Everyone always said Jonah looked like her. On that day she'd come home from work to find him lying facedown in bed, his cheeks and pillow stained with tears that had long since dried. Jonah came home four hours before his parents, so he always had time to cry alone.

She'd rubbed his back, her rings catching on his shirt. "What happened?"

Jonah spoke into his pillow. "They called me names. After school. Peter especially. The one I told you about." His voice cracked a little. "I shouldn't cry."

That's what his father always told him.

"It's okay to cry," his mother said comfortingly. "But not in front of the person who hurts you. What did he say?"

"I don't know," Jonah murmured. "He said my haircut was dumb. And that I had big ears. And that I looked like a girl. He was pretty busy. Lots to say, I guess."

His mother patted his back. "Here's what you do. Tomorrow he'll call you more names, right?"

"That seems to be the pattern," Jonah agreed.

"So this time you'll say, Very creative, Peter. I especially like the part about my dumb haircut. Can I use that one?"

Jonah glanced at her. "I'm not sure you're getting the problem."

She smiled. "I am. When someone doesn't like you, say something nice about them. It makes them angry, because it makes you better."

Jonah thought about that. "It's worth a try, I guess."

The next day he had told Peter that he liked his shoes, and Peter punched him in the stomach. As Jonah lay there, he decided that he was done taking advice from his mother. But the day after that, Peter didn't say anything. Maybe it wasn't as fun anymore. Maybe the principal had threatened to expel him. It was a private school, and they didn't like it when you punched other students.

But it had worked. And so Jonah decided to try it again.

To be fair, Lyana the Forgotten didn't punch him in the stomach. She just stared at him for a moment and then looked at Willona, who shrugged.

"Where did we find this kid?" Lyana said.

"I assume you don't actually want an answer," Willona replied, "because that's classified and I'd have to report you. You're probably just surprised because that was a little weird. I'll pretend you didn't ask." She paused. "We'll probably get going now."

"Good idea," Lyana said.

When they left the cafeteria, Willona turned to him. "You like her ribbons?"

"I thought it was a nice thing to say," Jonah mumbled.

"You are an Incredible Space Raider, Jonah," she said. "You don't have time for ribbons. And what's wrong with my hair?"

Jonah frowned. "Nothing. It's nice."

"Thank you," Willona said. "But it's too late. Now, we better go say good-bye to Alex. He's going to have to go deep into the Wild Zones. . . ." She stopped. "Uh-oh."

Jonah turned around and saw Erna the Strong walking toward them. Terrified Space Raiders pressed against the walls in front of her, trying to get out of her way.

"I'm in trouble," Jonah whispered.

Erna the Strong stopped in front of him. "Jonah the Now Incredible, you are summoned to Sector One. The commander would like a word."

"Do I have a choice?" Jonah asked.

"No," Erna said.

Jonah watched as more and more Space Raiders stepped into the hallway, closely watching the encounter. Ben the Brilliant was wearing a very evil-looking smirk. He spotted Jemma, and she just gave him a sad smile.

Jonah resigned himself to his fate. "Lead on," Jonah said.

"Actually, I walk behind you," Erna the Strong replied. "Regulations."

"Makes sense," Jonah said.

He started walking down Squirrel Street, Erna the Strong close behind him. Willona obviously couldn't resist. "Wait! Was he on the List?"

Erna the Strong hesitated. She probably wasn't supposed to say anything, but she could see that every single person in the sector was eagerly listening for the answer. Even Lieutenant Gordon had stepped out of his room. Erna the Strong couldn't resist.

"We don't know," she said. "Because the List was gone."

Everyone looked at Jonah, their eyes wide.

"Is that a bad thing?" he whispered to Willona.

She nodded. Erna the Strong turned back to him.

"I like your hair," Jonah murmured.

Erna raised one of those fierce, bushy red eyebrows, dug her incredibly strong fingers into his shoulders, and started pushing him down the hallway. He caught one last glimpse of Willona the Awesome, sadly waving good-bye.

CHAPTER EIGHT

"HOW DID YOU DO IT?" LIEUTENANT POTTS asked, leaning forward dramatically.

He was a round-faced boy with bright pink cheeks, deep-set blue eyes, and a nose that looked a bit like a pig's snout. He was also one of the few Space Raiders on the ship who wasn't wiry and slender; on the contrary, he had a bit of belly that hung out below the table. But despite his jolly appearance, he wasn't overly friendly. Actually, he was a bit of a bully. He was also the leader of Sector Two.

"Well?" he repeated.

Jonah looked around the room, confused. The commander was watching intently.

"How did I do what?" Jonah asked.

Lieutenant Potts sat back, shaking his head in exasperation. Samantha the Bravest and Most Daring Adventurer folded her arms, staring at him suspiciously.

"How did you steal the List?" she said. "How did you know where it was?"

She looked a lot like Alex, now that Jonah took a

better look at her. She had the same wispy blond hair that fell well past her shoulders, and equally big, round ears. He thought maybe she'd take pity on him, since he knew Alex, but apparently not.

Jonah wasn't exactly sure what to say. He was being accused of stealing something he'd never seen on a ship he'd been on for a day from a bunch of people who terrified him. Erna the Strong was waiting by the door, ready to take him back to the brig.

"I didn't steal anything," Jonah said. "I've only left Squirrel Street once so far. And then Alex and I ran into a screaming monster, so I wasn't in a rush to leave again."

The commander tapped a finger on the table. She seemed to like doing that.

"Is it possible he could have found the List without knowing where it was?"

Samantha seemed to think about that. "I guess. I found it by accident." She paused. "But it would have taken him a while."

"Is there any chance he could have slipped away for that long?" the commander asked Lieutenant Gordon, who had hurried along behind Jonah and joined the meeting.

Lieutenant Gordon shook his head. "I don't think so. When we lost Kyla the Courageous and Daniel the Ninja, he was sent back to his room. But the guards were still at their stations. He couldn't have left."

Lieutenant Potts snorted. "How convenient."

Jonah put up his hand.

The commander looked at him in surprise. "Yes?"

"Can I speak without being sent to the brig?" Jonah asked.

"That depends," she replied.

Jonah lowered his hand uncertainly. "Can I just say that I hoped Samantha would find the List and prove that I'm not an Incredible Space Raider? I don't want to be here either. I want to go home."

Everyone looked at the commander. Lieutenant Gordon rubbed his forehead.

The commander stared at Jonah for what seemed like a very long time. Her lightning-streaked hair was tied into a ponytail this time, revealing her sharp cheekbones.

"You can't go home, Jonah the Now Incredible," she said finally. "Not until our mission is done." She looked around the room. "We can't blame him for wanting to go home. But in the absence of proof, we have to assume he was recruited for the ISR."

Lieutenant Potts looked like he was going to object, but he thought better of it.

The commander turned back to Jonah. "I don't think you stole the List, Jonah. You don't seem . . . quite capable of that. No offense."

"None taken," Jonah said.

She nodded. "However, if you are the right recruit,

then you are also a special recruit. We don't know why that is, but perhaps we'll find out soon. For now, we're in a serious situation. You can return to training and be granted some information about our mission. You are still, however, on brig duty."

"We can't give information to a possible spy," Lieutenant Potts said.

The commander straightened and looked at him. Jonah heard Erna the Strong shift behind him. Lieutenant Potts shrank in his chair.

"I believe I just said Jonah was a member of the ISR," the commander said quietly. "Didn't I say that?"

Everyone in the room nodded.

"I thought so," she continued. "Does that mean you're questioning my judgment, Lieutenant Potts?"

"No," he said quickly, his round pink cheeks turning bright red. "Sorry."

She held his gaze for a moment longer and then turned to Lieutenant Gordon. "You will inform your sector that Jonah is cleared for duty. Jonah, you are dismissed. You can take him back, Erna."

With that, Erna the Strong escorted him out, a little more gently this time. He felt Lieutenant Potts watching him go. Jonah suspected he hadn't seen the last of him.

When they were back in the hallway, Erna the Strong looked at him.

"You're lucky," she said.

"I guess," Jonah agreed. "Can you grab my arms? My shoulders kind of hurt."

Erna the Strong smiled, the first time she'd done so. "You're not in trouble, Jonah the Now Incredible. You can walk on your own." She paused. "But I still walk behind you."

Jonah nodded. "Fair enough." He started down the hallway. "Do you think they'll be nicer to me now?"

There was another pause. "No."

Erna the Strong was right. They all stared at him coldly when he walked back into the sector, a free Space Raider. Willona came out of her bedroom and looked at him in shock. She must have thought he was never coming back, unless it was to go straight to the brig. Even when Lieutenant Gordon came back and told everyone that Jonah was an official member of the ISR, it didn't change. They all kept staring.

Before long, Jonah found himself back in his bedroom. It was small and cold and the view of space was a bit lonely, but it was better than being out there with the others. Even Jonah, who was used to getting teased, could only take so many dirty looks before he needed a break. And so he just sat there on his tiny cot with its very thin white pillow stained yellow, brown blanket with loose threads and holes, and sheets that probably hadn't been washed in twenty years. He stared out the window at the lonely view of space and looked at the tiny stars and the great blackness that seemed to go on forever.

He missed his family. Even his sister. She was seventeen and very popular, which of course meant she had to be mean to Jonah. Or so he gathered. But she did have her moments. Once, she gave him a ride to school when he was late. And once, she told her boyfriend that he should stop calling him Jonie. That was nice. He missed her.

All of a sudden the window got blurry, and he realized he was crying. And then it hit him. He'd contracted space sadness. Willona had been right.

He picked up his journal. He had to fight it off.

Dear Mom and Dad . . . and Mara,

I know I already wrote you several letters (well, not you, Mara, but I did include you at the bottom in the first one), but I have contracted space sadness and have to write you another one. I suppose I could just write a journal entry, but that still feels weird.

I am now an official member of the ISR, and I have

not yet been eaten by the Shrieker. These are both technically good things, but I'm still sad. No one here likes me, and I think it's because I have parents. I don't really understand. At least Peter thought I looked like a girl. It made sense. But parents? It's very confusing.

They also confirmed that I'm a special recruit. That should also be a good thing, but it might also mean I have to fight the EETs first or something. That would be bad, since I still haven't practiced with my bonker. I better do that soon.

I know I already kind of said sorry, but I just wanted to say that again. I was thinking about Mara, and she does more nice things than I thought. Actually, I think I might have done as many mean things as her. Space makes you remember things. You know how she got home late and you caught her because something woke you up? That was me knocking on your door. I don't know why I did it. Maybe I was jealous that she was out and I was home playing video games. Oh, another time I put an old herring into her boyfriend's shoe for a few hours and then took it out just before he left, so he probably smelled like fish all day.

Anyway, tell her I'm sorry. But still not her boyfriend. Did they break up yet?

I don't know if this space sadness is deadly, but if so, this may be my last letter. If that is the case, good-bye.

Sincerely,
Jonah

Jonah did feel a little better. It was like he got to talk to someone who didn't want to exile him or throw him into the brig. That was a nice change.

However, he was still a bit lonely, and space kept rolling by his window. And so he was actually happy when there was a quiet knock at his door a few hours later.

"Hey," Willona said, looking at the floor. She held out a food bar. "You dropped this."

"Thanks," Jonah replied. He was very hungry. "Is everything all right?"

She glanced at him. "Yes. Well, no. Everyone thinks you're a spy. Possibly a superspy, since no one saw you leave and steal the List. Even me. And I was with you."

"Who would I be spying for?" Jonah asked.

She shrugged. "The crew. Maybe even the EETs."

"Why would I spy for evil aliens that are trying to destroy the universe?"

"Who knows?" Willona said. "Could be that they paid you off to infiltrate our ranks and sabotage our mission. For all we know, you are an EET. Well, I doubt that, since they're supposedly, like, eight feet tall and have claws and sharp teeth, but it is one theory. I mean, how else could you have snuck out and stolen the List? It seems impossible."

"That's because I didn't steal it," Jonah said.

"It's just a little suspicious," Willona replied. "You know—the guards disappear, and then the List is stolen. They think it might be an inside job."

Jonah frowned. "Who's 'they'?"

"Ben."

"He really doesn't like me," Jonah said. "Maybe I should talk to him."

"To tell him you like his shoes?" Willona asked.

Jonah hesitated. "I was going to say something nice."

Willona shook her head and walked into the room. "That doesn't work, you nincompoop. I still like you, Jonah. I know that I would probably like a superspy, since they would be very smooth, and girls always like spies."

"They do?" Jonah asked.

"I heard that once," Willona said. "But you seem so nice. And, you know, defenseless. No offense."

"None taken," Jonah muttered.

Willona turned to face him. "But it's hard, you know. This is my first career posting, and I don't want to mess it up. I'm on the rise. And people might think I'm helping out a spy. That can't be good."

Jonah nodded. He knew what was coming. He was sad, but he couldn't blame her. She had her career to think about. "So you can't be seen with me anymore."

She sighed. "I'm sorry."

"It's okay," Jonah said. "I understand."

"You're on brig duty," Willona said. "The lieutenant wanted me to tell you. Usually no one starts without training, but since your first job is to release Martin, the only prisoner, you're probably safe. I'll still bring you messages, but that's all. Sorry."

Jonah just nodded again. He actually felt like he might cry, but he held it back. He remembered what his mother said: Don't cry in front of the person who hurt you.

Willona was just leaving when she saw the journal and the pen on his cot. It was open to Jonah's letter. She stared at it for a moment, then looked at Jonah.

Without warning, she walked up to him and gave him a hug.

"No spy would get space sadness," she whispered, and then she pulled back again. Her eyes were watering. "Forget my career. I choose friends. Well, both. I still want a career. I'll just make them like you again. I am the third most important greeter. I got the job for my charm.

And because I can't use a bonker. I'll work on everyone else. Don't worry, Jonah. I'm here for you. Even if it looks lonely from your window."

She hurried out of the room, and Jonah smiled and wiped his eyes, just to be sure. Still dry. His parents would be proud.

Willona poked her head back into the room. "PS: You start right now."

CHAPTER NINE

THE CURRENT BRIG GUARD, A BOY NAMED ERIC the Excellent, gave Jonah a wary look as he stepped away from the door. He didn't seem to trust Jonah with the job.

"So I can let Martin out?" Jonah asked as Eric the Excellent slowly backed away, making sure to keep his eyes on Jonah while clutching his bonker.

That seemed to be the new strategy for the Space Raiders. They couldn't exile Jonah, but they certainly didn't trust him. They'd carefully watched him all the way down Squirrel Street, popping out of doorways and sending hand signals down the hall. Even now at least four armed Space Raiders were watching the exchange. Jonah wasn't exactly sure what damage he could do guarding what would soon be an empty brig, but lots of things didn't make much sense on the *Fantastic Flying Squirrel*. He was getting used to it.

"Yeah," Eric said cautiously, still backing away. "Lieutenant Gordon thought you might want to do it, since you've already done some hard time with Martin."

Jonah shrugged. "It was just three hours."

"For now," Eric said.

"So I just stand here?" Jonah called. Eric was already twenty feet away.

Eric reached his bedroom door. "Think you can manage it?"

Then he quickly stepped into his room and slammed the door shut. The loud clang echoed down Squirrel Street. Jonah just sighed and swung open the brig door. Light flooded into the small cell, pushing back the darkness. Jonah's eyes widened.

There, lying in the middle of the floor, was Martin the Marvelous.

He was lying flat on his back, eyes closed, arms sprawled out beside him. It looked like he'd been shot. Jonah rushed into the room and knelt down beside him.

"Martin," he said desperately, shaking his shoulders. "Martin!"

Martin's eyes flicked open. "Yes?"

Jonah yelped and fell backward in surprise. "Why are you on the floor?"

"I sleep here," Martin said calmly. "Good for your posture. And the bed smells."

Jonah shook his head and stood up. "Do you have to sleep like that?"

Martin slowly climbed to his feet, squinting against the light. "Always have. What did you do now?"

"Nothing," Jonah said. "You're free."

Martin looked out into the hallway. "I am?"

Jonah nodded. "I'm the brig guard now."

Martin gave Jonah a fierce hug. "Thank you! Thank you! It's been the longest three days of my life. From now on, Whiskerface is on his own. Or I'll just share my bar. Probably that. Poor Whiskerface. He's probably starving!"

Martin skipped out of the brig. "I'm back!" He came to an abrupt halt.

Jonah followed him out and saw that at least ten grim-looking Space Raiders were now watching them from all parts of Squirrel Street, their hands on their weapons.

Martin turned to Jonah. "Did I miss something?"

Martin the Marvelous headed off to his bedroom soon after, and Jonah was left alone, standing in front of the old, rusted brig door. He had no idea how long he was supposed to stand here, or if they even had clocks or time or night and day on the Squirrel.

He did know he was getting tired. On the way to his shift, he'd managed to quickly eat the food bar, which still tasted like bean-flavored cardboard. It was mealy and grainy and a dark brown color that was really unappetizing. But Jonah felt like he hadn't slept in days, with all the excitement since he'd been on the *Squirrel*, and he was really hoping his shift would be over soon.

The hours dragged on, and one Space Raider after another marched past, glaring at him and shaking their heads at his badge. He watched Alex head off down Death Alley to cheers and well wishes from the others, but Alex didn't say anything to Jonah.

The one bright spot was a quick visit from Jemma, who just gave him a warm smile and said, "Welcome to the ISR." Then she patted him on the arm and left again.

But other than that, he just stared at the gray metal wall in front of him, wondering how old the *Squirrel* was and where it came from and whether or not he would get another food bar when he was finished. Disgusting or not, he was getting hungry.

At one point, Ben the Brilliant walked by, looked at Jonah, and stopped, sneering. Jonah glanced nervously at the bonker in his hand. He really wished Alex had taught him some moves before he left.

"So you're an official member now," Ben said. He was even taller up close, at least four inches taller than Jonah.

"Yep," Jonah replied.

Ben met his eyes. "I don't know how you managed to trick the commander, but we're all watching you. If you make one wrong move, I'll kick your heinie."

"That's the same as 'keister', right?" Jonah asked, trying to remember.

"Don't play games with me," Ben said.

"What game?" Jonah asked.

Ben shook his head. "You think you're pretty clever, don't you? I think you're just a cow-headed grass face."

Jonah frowned. "Is that an insult?"

"What do you think, cloud brain?"

"I don't know anymore," Jonah said.

Ben leaned in. "You don't belong here."

Jonah took a tiny step backward. "Probably not."

Ben smiled, exposing particularly yellow teeth. His breath smelled like old food bars. "Are you scared, monkey head?"

"I will assume you're not talking to an on-duty Space Raider," Willona said suddenly, hurrying down Squirrel Street. "That would be against the rules, of course! Not good. Four hours in the brig, I think. Have to check the rules. Jonah might forget your bathroom break, too. Couldn't blame him."

Ben glanced at her. "Of course not. Just making sure he was all right." He gave Jonah one last sneer and then headed down the hallway.

Willona reached Jonah and smiled. "How was it?"

"Long," Jonah said. "Why is there a guard when the brig is empty, anyway?"

Willona seemed to think about that. "Rules," she said finally. "Getting tired?"

"Yeah," Jonah said. "Is it nighttime?"

"It's always nighttime in space. But it's time for you to sleep. You're on again when Eric the Excellent is tired.

You're the only two brig guards." She started down the hallway. "I have to go check on the Death Alley guards. I relieve them for bathroom breaks. Couldn't find work for me, now that I've greeted everyone. We do need to have a rules lesson soon, though. Maybe I'll wake you up a bit early. Oh, and get a food bar. It's almost time for breakfast!"

She stopped to knock on Eric the Excellent's door, yelled for him to wake up, and then gave Jonah one last lopsided grin before turning down Death Alley. Jonah waited until a groggy-looking Eric the Excellent poked his head out of his door, and then he headed for the cafeteria.

Lyana the Forgotten was sitting at a table when he walked in. She was just sitting there, twisting one of her long braids around her finger, staring at the wall.

"You're a bit early for breakfast," she said immediately.

"Oh," Jonah said. "Sorry. I just got off guard duty."

She stared at him for a moment and then went to grab him a food bar. She handed it to him, but when he grabbed it she held on to her end. Jonah looked at her, confused.

"I don't think you're a spy, Jonah," she said quietly.

Jonah looked away from her intent gaze. "Thanks. Me either."

"But you're not a Space Raider, either," she said.

"Oh," Jonah murmured.

He snuck another glance at her. Once again, he just saw sadness in her eyes.

"You're not a Space Raider because you're not afraid. And you're not afraid because you haven't felt pain," she whispered.

"Okay," Jonah said. He wanted to leave now. He could wait until lunch to eat.

Lyana smiled, but there was nothing happy or comforting about it. Jonah never knew a smile could be a sad thing. "And I feel bad for you," she said, letting go of the food bar. "Because when we get to the Dark Zone, you're going to be very, very afraid."

She turned and went back to her seat. Jonah stood there for a second, frowning, and then headed back to his room. He ate his food bar alone while the stars rolled past his window, wondering what Lyana had meant. Whatever she meant, she was wrong.

He was afraid.

He picked up his journal and wrote a very short letter.

Dear Mom and Dad and Mara,

I want to go home now.

Sincerely,
Jonah

Then he climbed beneath his thin, fraying blanket, put his head on that old, yellowing pillow, and fell asleep. He dreamed of a family dinner in the yard.

Jonah woke to a knock. He rolled over, still sleepy, but four more sharp raps later he groaned, crawled out of bed, and opened the door. As usual, it was Willona.

"Our lesson is canceled," she said quietly.

"Why?" Jonah asked.

She hesitated. "Alex didn't come back. Neither did the second most important adventurer. They were supposed to only go for a few hours. It's been nine."

She looked like she was on the verge of tears.

"Lieutenant Gordon has called a memorial service. Come on."

Jonah followed her down Squirrel Street. He kept thinking about Alex the Adventurer. How he might have been caught in the open with no grate to save him.

The Space Raiders had gathered in front of the lieutenant's office again, and Lieutenant Gordon stood at the front of them. This time the commander and Erna the Strong weren't there. Lieutenant Gordon gazed out at the assembled Space Raiders, looking grave.

"We meet here today in honor of Alex the Adventurer. The commander would have liked to join us, but the second most important adventurer didn't return either, so she's leading the service in Sector Two."

There was a concerned murmur through the crowd.

"She sent Samantha the Bravest and Most Daring Adventurer to find them, but she has also disappeared."

The murmurs grew louder. Jonah spotted Lyana the Forgotten watching from the edge of the crowd. She met eyes with Jonah, and he looked away.

The lieutenant held up his hands. "We have to remain calm. And before we can make plans, we need to honor our own adventurer. Alex was a hero, and we remember him as one." He put his hand on his badge. "May he raid in peace."

The rest of the Space Raiders did the same.

"Now," Lieutenant Gordon said, "we are currently working on plans—"

"Are we going to go look for them?" Eric the Excellent asked.

Lieutenant Gordon hesitated. "We don't know."

This caused an even larger stir.

"Why not?" Willona the Awesome asked.

Lieutenant Gordon looked at her. "Our adventurers are gone. Who wants to go into the Wild Zones to look for them?"

The Space Raiders fell silent. Jonah saw them glance at each other, and then at the floor. They all wanted to look for Alex the Adventurer. But no one wanted to go out there. They all knew the adventurers probably weren't coming back. Jonah glanced at Lyana.

He was afraid. No doubt about it. But everyone kept telling him he wasn't a real Space Raider, so he might as well be the one to leave. Besides, he liked Alex.

"I'll do it," Jonah said. His voice sounded very squeaky, even to his own ears.

Everyone turned to look at him in shock.

"What did you say?" Lieutenant Gordon asked, frowning at him.

"I said I'll do it," Jonah repeated. "I'll go look for Alex."

Lieutenant Gordon stared at him for a moment longer and then nodded.

"Get him a map."

CHAPTER TEN

THE SPACE RAIDERS GATHERED IN DEATH ALLEY to see Jonah off, though it wasn't quite as celebratory as when Alex left. Many were still scowling at him, while the rest just looked like they were already at his memorial service. He half expected them to put their hands on their badges and tell him to raid in peace. Jonah was definitely trembling now.

Jemma smiled at him from the crowd, but it wasn't as comforting as usual. Jonah suspected that she was saying a silent good-bye as well.

Jonah was terrified. No other way to put it. But it was too late to go back now. He was leaving with just a few items: a copy of Alex's map—which he somehow doubted was going to help—a bonker, and his notepad, which Willona said he should take in case he got trapped somewhere and wanted to record his thoughts. That was comforting.

Lieutenant Gordon appeared beside Jonah at the front of the gathering.

"We have gathered to see off Jonah the Now

Incredible, who has bravely volunteered to search for our missing adventurers," he said. "Now, I know some of you think we are just exiling him—"

Jonah glanced at the lieutenant, who ignored him.

"But that is not the case," Lieutenant Gordon continued. "He is on a top-level mission. And even if you think he's a spy, it would still be nice to wish him luck."

A hand in the crowd went up.

"Yes?" Lieutenant Gordon asked.

"If he's a spy," the boy said, "won't he just be returning to the crew to give them our secrets and doom us all?"

Everyone looked at Lieutenant Gordon, who seemed to think about that.

"Yes, probably," he said. "But we have already decided he's not a spy."

Another hand raised. Lieutenant Gordon nodded at her.

"If he comes back, shouldn't we assume he is a spy?" the girl asked.

Everyone looked at Lieutenant Gordon again.

"The commander said Jonah is not a spy," he said firmly. "And so if he comes back, he's just a heroic Space Raider who somehow managed to do what all our best adventurers could not. And hopefully he'll be able to explain how he did that."

Victoria the Avenger—the girl with the dimples—suddenly stepped out of the crowd and walked toward

Jonah. He looked at the lieutenant, who seemed equally confused. Victoria reached him and shyly met his eyes. Jonah felt himself flush.

"Can I ask you for a favor?" she murmured.

"Uh . . . yeah, sure."

"If you see my brother out there . . . will you bring him back? He has messy brown hair and dimples like me. His name is Matt the Amazing."

Her dark eyes were watering now, and she roughly wiped them.

Jonah knew he shouldn't promise anything. But he really, really wanted to.

"If I see him, I'll rescue him," Jonah said firmly. "I promise."

She smiled and squeezed his hand. "Thank you, Jonah the Now Incredible."

Lieutenant Gordon shifted uncomfortably. "Okay, that's enough . . . distractions. Jonah needs to get started." He turned to Jonah. "Are you ready?"

Jonah looked at the Space Raiders and then nodded. "I guess."

"Good," Lieutenant Gordon said. "Then let's—"

"Wait!"

The Space Raiders suddenly pulled apart, all looking back in surprise. There, standing with a bonker and a food bar, was Martin the Marvelous.

"I'm going with him," Martin said, walking through the group.

Lieutenant Gordon frowned. "This is a very dangerous mission—"

"We've done hard time together," Martin said. "And he freed me from the brig. He needs my help. I've been a criminal long enough. It's time to be a true Space Raider."

He stepped beside Jonah and nodded at him.

The Space Raiders were all talking among themselves now. Lieutenant Gordon looked skeptical, but he obviously decided that two adventurers were better than one.

"Then good luck to both of you," he said.

Jonah and Martin started down Death Alley, and the two guards parted to let them through. Jonah heard the whispers growing behind them as they reached the shadowy end of Death Alley, where it ran into the Haunted Passage. They both took a last look behind them and turned toward the Unknown Zone.

The ceiling lights flickered eerily as the empty hallway ran off into the darkness, and the groaning sounds of the *Squirrel*'s engine filled the air.

Martin looked at Jonah. "I should have stayed in the brig."

Jonah and Martin slowly walked down the Haunted Passage. Between the flickering light panels and the distant groaning of the *Squirrel's* engine, it felt like they were walking through a haunted castle like the ones Jonah had seen in films.

Martin ran his fingers along the metal as they went, looking around with wide brown eyes. His black hair was unkempt, like many of the Space Raiders, but he did have those sparkling white teeth that flashed when he spoke. Jonah had seen very few Space Raiders with good teeth. He assumed there weren't many toothbrushes in space.

They soon reached the blue door with the claw marks, and the two boys came to an abrupt halt. Martin just stood there, staring at it.

"It's true," he whispered.

The small, slender boy traced his fingers over the claw marks. Jonah did the same. The marks were about an inch deep into the metal and got even deeper as they ran along the door, as if the creature had kept pressing harder. More disturbingly, they were grouped together in threes. Whatever had made these marks didn't have five fingers.

"Do you know anything else about the Entirely Evil Things?" Jonah asked.

Martin shook his head. "Just that they got on board once. The story came from Sector One. Some say it was the commander who told it."

Jonah glanced up. Some of the scratches were near the top of the seven-foot door.

"So you're sure it wasn't the Shrieker?" he asked quietly.

Martin paused. "No, I'm not sure."

As Jonah continued to stare at the scratch-covered blue door, Martin inspected the control panel. Jonah tried to imagine what sort of creature could make these marks. He decided it was probably better that he didn't know. Particularly since he might have to fight it with a bonker in less than a month.

He glanced at Martin and saw that he was fiddling with the wires.

"What are you doing?"

"Trying something," Martin replied. He was carefully reattaching the wires by tying copper ends to one another. His thin little fingers were very deft and clever.

"Are you sure we want to go inside?" Jonah asked.

"Probably not," Martin said. "But I'm curious. It probably won't—"

He attached the last two wires, and the blue door slid open with a whoosh.

"Work," Martin murmured.

Jonah peered into the room. A few dusty old light panels had flickered on with the opening of the door, though they did little to pierce the shadows.

"Should we investigate?" Martin asked.

Jonah looked down the Haunted Passage, where the Unknown Zone was waiting.

"Why not?" he said resignedly.

The two boys walked into the shadowy room. It was as big as the cafeteria, but it contained no tables or counters or sink. The walls were covered in empty racks that looked like they might once have held guns. A few empty black crates were also pushed into the corners. But that wasn't all. There were cardboard boxes labeled RATIONS sitting on the floor, as well as various odds and ends. Martin picked up a faded gray shirt.

"I don't get it," Martin said.

Jonah walked around the room, lightly kicking a few other scattered pieces of clothing. He found old food-bar wrappers and even a bloodied bandage that he decided not to touch.

"Check this out," Martin said from across the room.

He was holding a stuffed pink monkey. It looked to be in relatively good condition, though Martin brushed some dust off its pink fabric. The monkey was wearing a big smile, which Jonah found a bit ironic, since it had been stuck in this eerie room.

"I was going to say it looked like Space Raiders were stuck in here," Martin said thoughtfully. "But they're not very tough Space Raiders if one had a pink monkey." He paused. "It is pretty soft, though. Think they would make fun of me if I brought it back?"

"Probably," Jonah said.

Martin sighed. "Yeah, you're right." He reluctantly put the monkey down again.

"Well, we should probably keep moving," Jonah said. "We have to—"

He stopped midsentence.

"What?" Martin asked.

Jonah had spotted something tucked behind one of the empty crates. He quickly crossed the room and bent down to retrieve it. It was a small black notebook.

He glanced at Martin and opened it. There were only two entries, both written by an unsteady hand. Jonah stood up and started reading.

Dear Diary,
I didn't have a chance to get you before they came. Maybe I can glue these pages in if we get out. I don't know if we will. We're trapped in here. Father tells me we're going to be okay, but he looks scared. We heard the scratching. It sounded like they would get in. I screamed and cried, and the other men told me to be quiet.

Then the scratching stopped. We heard breathing and footsteps and something like voices. I keep Mr. Monkey close, but he's the only one who smiles now.

I don't know what they are. But they're on the ship, and we're stuck in this room. I wish Mother was here.

Signed,
the space princess

Jonah glanced at Martin. "Do you know who the space princess is?"

He shook his head. Jonah read the second entry.

Dear Diary,
It's been two days. I didn't write because the scratching started again. We heard it from the ceiling this time.

Jonah immediately looked up, then continued reading.

We haven't heard anything all day. No footsteps or scratching or anything at all. The men are talking about leaving. We don't have any water. Father keeps looking at me while they talk. They say the outside door panel is broken. Once it closes, they won't be able to get back in for a while. That means I have to go with them. I don't know if I'll be coming back.
I'm so scared. I miss you, Mom.
Signed,
the space princess

Jonah closed the diary and looked at Martin. "She never came back for Mr. Monkey."

"Yeah," Martin said quietly. "Or the diary entries."

Jonah gently put the notebook back where it was. "We should go."

Martin nodded and started for the door. "I don't like this room."

He was just stepping into the hallway when the first cackling laugh flooded down the Haunted Passage. A shrieking voice filtered along behind it, and just like the first time, it grew louder and louder as they carried down the hall. The Shrieker was back.

Martin looked at Jonah in terror.

"The door," Jonah said, grabbing Martin and pulling him back into the room.

The cackling, inhuman laughter grew louder, and Jonah smacked the inside door panel with the palm of his hand. Thankfully it still worked, and the blue door slid shut.

Slapping feet ran by the door in a flash, the shouting and laughter just inches away through the blue steel. Beside him, Martin just trembled and stood there as if he didn't dare move, his eyes fixed on the door.

Finally the Shrieker was past again, its voice echoing from farther down the Haunted Passage, and Martin looked at Jonah.

"Can we go back now?"

Jonah paused. He wanted to, but they couldn't give up already.

"No," he said. "Not until we find Alex."

Martin sighed. "I was afraid you were going to say that."

CHAPTER ELEVEN

JONAH AND MARTIN WAITED UNTIL THE Haunted Passage was completely silent again and then crept back into the hallway. Martin bent down to examine the floor.

"No footprints," he whispered. "Maybe it's a ghost."

"It's a metal floor," Jonah said. "Why would there be footprints?"

Martin seemed to think about that, and then stood up again. "Fair enough." He glanced at Jonah. "What now?"

Jonah nodded down the hallway. "We keep moving. I have a plan."

The two boys tiptoed down the Haunted Passage, keeping their backs pressed against the cool metal walls. Everything was cold on the *Squirrel*, as if space were constantly creeping through the ship's hull. Jonah could feel it through his uniform.

"Do you know Ben the Brilliant well?" Jonah asked.

Martin shrugged. "Sort of. We don't talk much. Why do you ask?"

"Just curious why he hates me so much."

"Because he's had a bad life," Martin said.

Jonah slowed down and looked back at Martin. "What do you mean?"

"Space Raiders usually talk when they first get to the ship. You know, about where they came from. I mean, most of Sector Three woke up at the same time. They scooped us all up and dumped us in the rooms. So we all wandered out, confused, and there was Lieutenant Gordon to welcome us all. He's actually from Sector One; the commander assigned three strong recruits to lead each of the other three sectors."

Jonah frowned. "So no one knew why they were here?"

"Of course not. The lieutenant gave us the history and then assigned us jobs. But we were all a little scared at first, obviously. Not me so much—I was used to scary places. But a lot of people were, and in the first few days it was hard to enforce the rules. Everyone was talking and swearing and forgetting to go to guard duty. Some were even wandering off into the ship, like Matty. But they didn't come back, and we realized it was time to start becoming Space Raiders."

Jonah looked around as they slowly crept down the hall. It was still silent.

"So what happened to Ben?"

Martin hesitated. "He only had his mom. I guess his dad was gone already. His mom worked in a factory. They didn't have a lot of money, I guess. Well, one day she got killed in an accident, when Ben was twelve. They came to get him, and they took him to the orphanage kicking and screaming and refusing to go. His grandparents were long dead. He ran away again and again and wouldn't let anyone adopt him or even speak to him. They put him in juvenile detention when he was thirteen. Finally got out a year later, but he just stayed at the orphanage, and they had nowhere to put him. He thinks he got picked to join the ISR because he has no one left to care about."

"So why does he hate me?" Jonah asked.

Martin met his eyes. "Because you do. Think about it: He's been seeing other kids with their families for years, and thinking how lucky they are. Coming here was his chance to be lucky. To be special. He thinks that you're taking that away from him."

Jonah looked away, his stomach twisting. It made sense. Suddenly Ben didn't seem like such a bully. Just a boy who wanted to be special.

"And what about you?" Jonah asked quietly.

Martin grinned. "I think being special has nothing to do with where you came from."

They soon reached the metal grate that Jonah and Alex had climbed into the first time they'd come to the Haunted Passage, when the Shrieker had almost gotten them. While they were hunkered inside, Jonah had noticed that the small, dusty air duct kept going behind him. He hadn't mentioned it then because he was afraid Alex would want to explore it, but Jonah guessed that those air ducts might run through the entire ship. If he was right, then that was their best chance to make it to the Unknown Zone alive. Jonah bent down and pulled the metal grate off.

"We're going to crawl in there, aren't we?" Martin asked miserably.

"Yep," Jonah said. "After you."

Martin made a face and then crawled into the air duct. Jonah followed him in, pulling the grate shut behind him. It clanged back into place.

Martin looked back. "Sorry you have my keister in your face."

"Just start crawling," Jonah replied.

Martin nodded and began crawling down the air duct. "This is pretty clever. Were you an adventurer back home?"

"Not really," Jonah said, grimacing at the dust beneath his hands. "You?"

"Sort of," Martin said. "I did a lot of sneaking."

Martin stopped as another duct opened up beside them, running left, along the Haunted Passage. The duct was dark and dusty and smelled like stale mothballs, and it disappeared into the shadows in the distance.

"That's the one we want," Jonah said.

"You sure about this?" Martin asked.

"No," Jonah said. "But I don't have any better ideas."

"Rats," Martin grumbled.

Jonah assumed that was another fake swear word. It reminded him of something as they started crawling again. "Does Whiskerface live in these air ducts?"

"I don't know," Martin said. "If he does, I hope he's the only rat in here. Most rats aren't as nice as Whiskerface. I think he thinks he's a cat. He even purrs. Kind of."

"Do you know a lot of rats?" Jonah asked.

Martin glanced back. "I did."

As they crawled along the duct, they soon passed another one on their left that looked like it ran back out and connected with the Haunted Passage. Jonah guessed that they were crawling through a main supply duct and they would find lots of little outlets back to the hallway as they went, where the recycled air filtered back to the main areas.

"How are we going to know when we get to the Unknown Zone?" Martin asked.

"I have no idea," Jonah replied. "I assume it will be completely dark and full of shrieking and laughter."

"Oh," Martin said.

They kept crawling. The main supply duct was only about two feet high and two feet wide, and Jonah was feeling a little cramped. It didn't help that Martin kept kicking up dust that billowed into his face. He was starting to feel like a rat himself.

"What's your job on the ship?" Jonah asked.

"When I'm not in the brig, hall guard," he said.

"Are you good with a bonker?"

"Not really," Martin replied. "You?"

"I don't think so."

Martin glanced back. "Then we better not run into the Shrieker. I'd like to know a few more moves, like Alex—"

"Shh," Jonah said suddenly. "Listen."

They both stopped. There were voices coming from the Haunted Passage. Human voices. Jonah and Martin exchanged a look.

"Get to the next grate," Jonah whispered.

Quickly crawling down the duct until they came to another opening, they crept up to the metal grate. The voices were growing louder. They didn't sound like Space Raiders.

"—running around everywhere. Going to mess something up, I'll tell you that much. Second one I've locked up today. And I still haven't heard from Grouter."

Jonah and Martin exchanged a look.

"The crew," Martin mouthed.

Jonah crawled forward to try to get a look. He could only really see silhouettes through the grate, but he could see the shapes of two grown men walking toward them.

"Gonna fill up the brig soon," a second man said, his voice gruff and deep. "Have to make a second one."

"Or shoot 'em into space," the first replied, chuckling. His voice was raspy and higher pitched. "Think the captain will agree?"

The second man laughed. "Doubt it. Rules are rules. Don't want to lose the contract."

The men were past now, walking farther down the Haunted Passage, toward Death Alley. Jonah hoped the guards would hear them coming and hide.

"Well, if they keep getting in my way, I'm gonna keep locking 'em up," the first man said. "And they won't like it in there with Leppy. I'll tell you that much."

"Who would?" the second man said. "I wish we could catch the shouter. That's the one I want."

The first man snorted. "You'll never catch 'im. Been trying for two years."

Their voices were getting fainter. Jonah strained to listen.

"Let's get back," the first man said. "We need to find Grouter."

Jonah just caught the name Grouter, and then it went silent.

He glanced at Martin. "We better get back. I think we know what happened to our adventurers."

Jonah thought about the conversation as they crawled back down the air duct. Who was Grouter? And Leppy? And why was Captain White Shark and his crew taking

Space Raiders? Something strange was going on in this ship, and he wanted to know what it was.

Martin had plenty of theories.

"Captain White Shark is evil," Martin explained. "He owns the ship, but he hates Space Raiders. Earth just hired him to take us to the Dark Zone. Maybe he works with the Entirely Evil Things." He paused. "This could all be a trap."

"But weren't there other Space Raiders before us?" Jonah asked.

"Yep," Martin said. "We're the seventh batch. The first six batches are already fighting the war somewhere in the Dark Zone. We haven't won yet, but I bet that will change when we get there. Me and you are going to bonk them right out of the galaxy."

Jonah thought about that. He wondered if the others would accept him as a real Space Raider now. He hoped so. He still wanted to go home, but the commander had made it clear that the *Squirrel* wouldn't go back to Earth until the mission was done. If that was the case, it would be nice if everyone stopped staring at him like they wanted to hit him with a bonker.

He led Martin back into the Haunted Passage and carefully closed the metal grate behind them. He didn't want the crew or the Shrieker to know about their secret tunnel.

"Isn't it strange that only the blue door has a control panel?" Martin asked. "None of these other doors have them, or any of the ones in Sector Three."

"Most things are strange on the *Squirrel*."

They were approaching the scratched blue door, which they'd left open. Jonah had wanted to close it to cover their tracks, but he figured the Space Raiders might want to investigate the room further and didn't want to risk closing it and losing the evidence if it didn't open again.

"Think they'll give us an extra food bar as a reward?" Martin asked, walking ahead. "I mean, we deserve it. We just journeyed into the Wild Zones and did some pretty good spying. Whiskerface has got to be getting hungry—"

They were just a few feet from the blue door when Jonah saw it: a pale shadow in the doorway. Someone was waiting for them.

"Look out!" he shouted.

But he was too late. A pair of large, hairy hands reached out from the doorway and grabbed Martin's collar. A barrel-chested man with a thick brown beard stepped out, holding a squirming, wriggling Martin. A second man with a thin, weasellike face and a cruel smile emerged behind him.

"Save yourself!" Martin shouted.

Jonah sprinted back down the Haunted Passage as the second man tried to grab him, and he heard heavy footsteps chasing after him. Jonah ran as fast as he could, not daring to look back.

"Leave him!" the other man shouted. "He'll come back eventually."

The footsteps stopped, and Jonah just kept running until he finally spotted the air duct and scrambled inside. He closed the grate behind him and sat there, trembling.

What was he going to do now?

CHAPTER TWELVE

JONAH SAT THERE FOR WHAT FELT LIKE HOURS, thinking about what to do next. He had three major problems. One was that those two crew members could still very well be waiting for him in the blue-door room. The second was that even if he could sneak by, he would be returning to Sector Three without Martin the Marvelous. Considering he had already been labeled a possible spy and traitor, he guessed that returning without his companion would not go over well.

And the final and most important problem was that he couldn't just leave Martin behind. Martin had come along to help Jonah, and now he was in the clutches of the crew. And since Jonah now knew that they were keeping their prisoners in a brig, he wasn't sure he could stand to say "may they raid in peace" and then go on as if the missing Space Raiders had never been there. No. As much as Jonah wanted to go back and the mere thought of anything else made his stomach turn, he had no choice.

He had to save Martin.

Jonah perched himself on all fours and started crawling through the air duct.

He thought back to Alex's map. The Haunted Passage and Squirrel Street were on the bottommost level of the Squirrel. There were five levels in all, with the top one being Captain White Shark and his crew's realm. That's where he needed to go.

Jonah looked down in disgust as the dust billowed around his hands. It was thick and dry, and at certain points his fingers hit areas where it was an inch thick. He just wrinkled his nose and kept crawling. Jonah soon reached the spot where he and Martin had overheard the discussion about someone named Grouter and the missing kids. This time he kept going.

But Jonah soon ran into a problem. About twenty feet ahead, the air duct suddenly veered straight upward and disappeared into the shadows. There was no way to climb it. Jonah sighed. He would have to venture back into the Haunted Passage.

Turning around in the cramped air duct proved difficult. He slid his legs up the vertical shaft and then slowly rolled onto his stomach. He felt his cheek brush against the dusty metal floor and tried not to think about what Alex had told him about the dead human skin cells. Clambering onto all fours, Jonah crawled back to the nearest air grate and cautiously popped it open. Even the faint scraping noise of detaching metal echoed through the ominous corridor. He took a quick look both ways, put the grate down, and climbed out.

The Haunted Passage looked much the same as it did farther down the ship. The walls were still gray and rusted and lined with doors, the floor was still worn down and stained with grease, and the ceiling panels still flickered with a pale, eerie light. But the groaning, moaning sounds of the *Squirrel*'s engines were far louder, and Jonah knew he must be getting close to the Unknown Zone: the home of the Shrieker.

His stomach did another little flop.

Jonah spotted more grates up ahead. While he was out here, he figured he might as well investigate.

He slowly walked down the Haunted Passage, inspecting the walls and doors and listening very carefully for shrieks and manic laughter. The doors were all very similar. Most were gray, while a few were red and one was even yellow. He did notice with interest and a bit of alarm that a few of them had scratches in the metal. Not as long or deep as the blue door, but definitely scratches. The creatures had been here, too.

He was just about to start looking for another grate when he noticed one gray door with a very small difference: a little symbol carved into the bottom corner. It said SP.

He knelt down to have a closer look. This symbol had been carved with a knife or tool; it hadn't chewed into the metal like the claw marks. A human had put the symbol here.

Jonah stood up and tried the door, expecting it to be locked. To his surprise, it slid right open, not even catching and straining like Jonah's door in Sector Three.

This one had been oiled.

A few light panels flickered on as he opened the door, and Jonah quickly stepped inside and shut the door. He didn't want any crew members stumbling upon him. Once it was firmly shut, he turned around and had a good look at the room.

It was a cafeteria with tables and chairs and a counter and a sink, but it was also completely littered with toys. Some sort of playhouse stood in the corner, a little pink house with white shutters and fake grass and plants bordering the doorway. Someone had even drawn a smiling yellow sun on the wall behind the house—barely visible against the dull gray metal—and white fluffy clouds around it. Jonah saw stuffed animals and dolls scattered on the floor and sitting up on the tables with teacups and plates of plastic food. But that wasn't all.

Empty glasses were lined up on the counter beside the sink, along with a few stacks of food bars. A garbage bin sat on the floor, full of silver wrappers. On one of the cupboards, someone had written *home sweet home* in a pink marker.

Then it hit him.

SP. The space princess. This used to be her playroom.

Jonah went to the counter to get himself a food bar and a glass of water. He figured now might be a good time for a break, since he was about to try to rescue captured Space Raiders from an evil captain and his crew and all. So he sat down, pulled his journal out of his pocket, and started writing.

Dear Mom and Dad and Mara,

I am currently trapped in the Haunted Passage, and my companion was just abducted by an evil space crew member. I have now decided to go rescue him and the rest of the captured Space Raiders. You're probably thinking that Jonah the baby would never do these things, but I seem to be more heroic in space. Probably because I have no choice. This place is full of evil things, and there's no time to be cowardly.

I think I had too much space sadness to ask this before, but did you know they were taking me? Did they ask you? Did you want to get rid of me? I hope you didn't, though the more time I spend in space, the more I realize how bad it was that I left my clothes on the floor and always forgot to take out the garbage and called Mara ugly.

And now I just thought of something. If you did want to give me up, then I am an orphan, and that's why the Space Raiders chose me. Maybe I belong here after all. Now I'm getting space sadness again.

Jonah sat back for a moment, staring down at the page. This was a disturbing thought. But he decided he couldn't end on a bad note. It wasn't very formal.

Never mind. I will just assume you didn't know and are sad, since if you are reading this letter I've probably been eaten and I'll never know anyway. And so I just wanted to say I love you and I'm sorry for the bad things I did and I know I am very lucky. You were a very good family.

I just wasn't always a very good boy.

Sincerely,
Jonah

Jonah closed the journal and took a last bite of his food bar. He grimaced.

He thought about what he'd written. His parents couldn't have given him up, could they? His mother had kissed him on the forehead the very morning Jonah was abducted, right before she went to work. Unless it was a good-bye kiss. Did she usually kiss his forehead? Yes, but she had also stroked his hair. Was she saying good-bye before they took him? It was impossible to be sure.

He tried to think back to the last time he'd seen his father.

His father was sitting on the couch, reading something on his tablet. He was wearing his brown housecoat and matching slippers, and his thinning salt-and-pepper hair was still slicked back from work. Jonah was watching the projector—he remembered that. But what were his father's last words to him? Jonah's eyes widened.

"Turn that down," his father had said, not even lifting his eyes from the tablet.

Those were his last words to Jonah. Had he annoyed his father so much that he gave him up? Why hadn't he just turned it down without being asked? He knew his father didn't like it that loud. Jonah started putting the pieces together. He'd annoyed his father, and after he'd gone to bed, his father had convinced his mother to give him up. She had argued, maybe, but ultimately agreed and then kissed him good-bye, knowing full well that the Incredible Space Raiders would snatch him up that very afternoon. It was a stretch, but yet here he was, sitting on a spaceship.

He was busy remembering all the other bad things he'd done when he noticed the empty glass sitting beside him on the table. A silver wrapper from a food bar lay beside it, surrounded by crumbs.

But much more important, there was also a little spill of water under the glass.

Jonah frowned. The air was dry and musty and cool, but water would still evaporate over time. He slowly walked over and touched the spilled water.

It was still cold.

Which meant the glass had been filled recently. Maybe that very day.

He glanced back at the door, suddenly alarmed. He'd assumed that journal was old and that the space princess and her father and Mr. Monkey had been trapped in the room with the blue door, hiding from those creatures, many, many years ago.

But now that he thought about it, he didn't know that. The space princess could still be on board. And that meant she could come back at any moment.

Jonah quickly filled a glass of water and chugged it down. Then he stuffed a few more food bars into the pockets of his uniform and reluctantly headed for the door. It would have been nice to spend a few hours in Home Sweet Home. It had stuffed toy frogs and teacups. But things were never easy on the *Fantastic Flying Squirrel.*

Jonah slowly slid the door open and risked a quick peek into the hallway. It was empty, so he stepped out, shut the door, and continued down the Haunted Passage. He was very confused. The space princess had to be a little girl, judging by the toys.

How was she avoiding the Shrieker? Was she a crew member's daughter?

He was still thinking about that when he came across something very, very disturbing. Jonah stopped midstep, his eyes widening. He'd found another open door.

Sort of.

It was a plain gray door, or used to be. The same kind that led into Jonah's bedroom back in Sector Three. In fact, there was a bedroom behind this one too. But it was the door that had Jonah trembling.

There were claw marks, but only on the few sections that were left. The rest had literally been torn open. The metal was stretched and torn and jagged, and a huge hole had been ripped in the middle where something large could squeeze its way inside.

Whatever it was—the Shrieker or the EETs—could rip doors open.

The blue door must have been reinforced, which made sense if they kept guns in there. Normal doors—the kind on every Space Raider's bedroom—didn't stand a chance.

He just hoped no one was in there at the time.

Jonah decided he was ready to head back into the air ducts. There were fewer signs of monsters in there.

He climbed into the nearest grate and saw that it led to a main supply duct that ran alongside the Haunted Passage, just like farther down the hall.

It was just as dusty and dark, too.

Sighing, Jonah started crawling down the duct, his fingers sliding on the dust. It occurred to him that if the space princess was still on the ship and still a kid playing with dolls, then it couldn't have been that long ago that the creatures attacked. Which meant they might very well still be on the ship.

He was definitely staying out of the Haunted Passage.

Jonah was still thinking about the claw marks as he turned left into the main duct. He stopped. There, crawling right toward him, was a girl.

She saw him and came to an abrupt halt. "Uh-oh," she said.

CHAPTER THIRTEEN

BEFORE JONAH COULD SAY ANYTHING, THE girl started backing down the air duct with surprising speed.

"Hey!" Jonah said. "Wait!"

She ignored him.

Jonah started crawling after her. "Wait!"

He chased her down the air duct, slowly closing in. He should have caught up quickly, considering she was moving backward, but she was clearly an experienced air-duct adventurer. She kept shooting annoyed glances at him as he called out for her.

The chase continued for another minute, until she finally backed past a supply duct and then crawled head-first toward the Haunted Passage. Jonah picked up his pace. If she got out of the air duct and ran, he would never catch her.

"This is really unnecessary!" he called, pumping his arms and legs.

He turned down the supply duct and saw that she was almost at the grate. From this angle he noticed she was wearing blue jeans and dirty sneakers. She clearly wasn't a Space Raider. The girl spared another annoyed look back at him. Jonah thought she might just push the grate off and run, but she was too careful. She was forced to pause for a moment, listening for footsteps and taking a peak out into the Haunted Passage.

She waited just a second too long.

Just as she was removing the grate and crawling out, Jonah took a desperate lunge and grabbed on to her right ankle. It wasn't very polite, but he was desperate. She tried to kick him off, but he held on tight, even as her left foot kicked him in the forehead.

"Ow," Jonah said. "Can you just wait a second? I need advice. I need to save the other Space Raiders."

The girl stopped kicking and looked back. "You're going to the top level?" she asked. She had a fairly thick British accent.

"That's the plan," Jonah said. "If I let go, will you kick me?"

She seemed to consider this. "I guess not."

Jonah tentatively let go, half expecting her to kick him in the head and run. Thankfully, she just slowly climbed to her feet and stood back, letting him crawl out of the air duct and stand up. She was a few inches taller than he was and probably a couple of years older. He saw now that she was wearing a purple woolen sweater over her ripped blue jeans. Both were stained. Even though her black hair was filthy and clumped together, it fell to her shoulders and framed delicate cheekbones and brown eyes. Her skin was the same light brown as Martin's. She looked almost regal—in a dirty, stuck on an old, musty ship kind of way.

It suddenly clicked into place.

"You must be the space princess," Jonah said, almost in awe.

She looked at him for a moment and then laughed. "The space princess? What have you been eating, dim-wit?" She didn't really speak like a princess. "You must be Prince Rat Boy, crawling through the ship to save me."

"Uh," Jonah said, confused. "No."

"Sally Malik," she said, extending her hand. "Fellow space rat."

Jonah tentatively shook her hand. She had a very strong grip, and he winced a little. "Jonah the Now . . . Jonah Hillcrest. What are you doing on this ship?"

She looked down the Haunted Passage. "This isn't the best spot. Follow me."

Without waiting for him to agree, Sally Malik took off down the hallway, moving with light, almost silent foot-steps. Jonah felt clunky and awkward behind her. They must have been close to the engine by now, as the moan-ing noise was even louder and there was a slight vibration in the floor. Jonah listened carefully for shrieking.

They walked by one double door with a button next

to it on the wall and a little blank screen over the doorway. Jonah knew what that was. An elevator shaft.

"Have you ever—"

"It's broken," Sally said, not even bothering to look back.

She stopped in front of a yellow door, which had faded and was exposing some of the rusted gray metal beneath it. Sally quickly pulled the door open and gestured for him to get inside. It was pitch black.

"Go," she said sharply.

Jonah hurried inside, and she shut the door behind them. Jonah couldn't see an inch in front of his face. He heard Sally's quiet footsteps move around him.

"You're not going to bonk me, are you?" he whispered.

She snorted. "You'd already be bonked."

There was a click, and a portable light flicked on and bathed the small room in a white glow. Jonah blinked against the sudden glare. They were in some sort of storage room, and it was filled with cleaning supplies and spare lights and tools and other odds and ends stacked on metal shelves. There was also a chair in the corner with some food bars and a bottle of water tucked beneath it.

"Welcome to my secret lair," Sally said, plunking down in the chair.

"It's nice," Jonah said hesitantly. "You sleep here?"

She frowned. "Of course not, bucket head. Do you see a bed in here? I have a little cot tucked in a service shaft near the back of the ship. In the Unknown Zone."

"You live in the Unknown Zone?" Jonah asked incredulously.

Sally nodded. "As long as you avoid the Shrieker, it's the safest place on the ship. The crew doesn't go there very much. Once in a while to fix engine problems, but you can always tell when that's going to happen. We stop moving."

Jonah found an old container of what looked like floor cleaner and sat down on it.

"How long have you been on the *Squirrel*?" Jonah asked.

Sally scooped up a food bar, opened the wrapper, and took a bite. She chewed a bit loudly, and she was still chewing as she replied. Definitely not a princess, he decided. "Must be two years by now," she said thoughtfully. "Or close to that. Hard to keep track of time on this old tub. It was the first batch, anyway. Want one?"

Jonah shook his head. "You were a Space Raider?"

"Once," she said, picking her teeth. "But I ran away."

"You what?"

She glanced at him. "I ran. I didn't want to fight Entirely Evil Things. I didn't even want to be a Space Raider. So I left, and I've been hiding in the ship ever since."

She finished her food bar and threw the wrapper in a bucket beside her.

"The commander tried to find me for a while. She and I were close. I was one of the first recruits. From Earth. Even after the first mission, she still sent adventurers after me. But it's hard to find a space rat. I thought someone had finally pulled it off today." She gave him a toothy grin. "But I guess it takes a rat to find one."

Jonah didn't particularly like being called a rat, especially after having the name Jonah the Now Incredible, but he supposed that was the least of his problems.

"So what do you do?" he asked.

She gestured around the room. "Hide. Eat. Sometimes I hang out in Home Sweet Home. I crawl around air ducts. Sleep in my room. Hide from the Shrieker and the crew. And mostly I sit up in the Bubble, staring at the stars. The one good thing about the *Fantastically Awful Flying Squirrel*."

"The Bubble?"

"I'll show you sometime . . . . if we meet up again."

Jonah frowned. "If?"

"I work alone," Sally Malik said. "Secret of my success."

She stood up, brushing some crumbs off her thick sweater.

"On that note, you should probably get moving. There's a main staircase farther down the hall, but watch out for crew members. The service shafts might be a better choice." She walked right past Jonah and opened the door. "See you, space rat. Maybe."

Jonah looked at her. He was slightly hurt that even a space rat didn't want him around. Sally seemed a bit rude and probably wouldn't have been the nicest companion, but it certainly beat sneaking through the *Squirrel* alone. But there was something she'd said that bothered him even more. Something he definitely didn't want to hear: She'd been here for two years.

"Why haven't you gone home?" he asked quietly.

"Home?" she said. Her dark eyes tightened and her voice lowered. "Home is a London street. But you're right. I would love to go back. I would love to feel the cold rain on my face and summer nights and hard stone and even those stiff little beds in the shelter when it's too cold to stay outside. But I can't. Once you're on the *Squirrel*, you're stuck. Maybe Space Raiders go home. I don't know. None of my friends did. They went off to the Dark Zone and never came back. Do yourself a favor—don't go back to the sectors. You're better off finding yourself a bed. The *Squirrel* is your home now."

Jonah thought of his mom and dad and Mara. He thought of his own bed and his own room. That was his home. And now she was telling him he could never go back.

Jonah felt his eyes water. He wasn't supposed to cry in front of the person who hurt him. But what did it matter now?

"Oh, here we go," Sally muttered. "Listen, it's not all bad. I mean, it's pretty bad. Actually, it's terrible. It's cold and dark and it sounds like a haunted house." She paused. "I'm not very good at this. Do you want a hug or something?"

Jonah shook his head and wiped his eyes with his sleeve. Then he stood up and nodded at her. "See you around," he said. "Maybe."

He walked slowly past her into the corridor.

"Ugh, you are annoying," Sally muttered. "You look like a lost puppy. Just sadder and less cute. All right, I'll take you to the engine room. You can sneak up to the top level a lot easier through there. But that's it."

Jonah looked back. "Thanks—"

"Shut it," she said, pushing him out the rest of the way and sliding the door shut. "I'm only doing this because I'm picturing a lost puppy. Don't ruin it by talking. And follow my lead. If you get me eaten by the Shrieker, I'm going to be very upset."

She started down the Haunted Passage.

"I like your sweater," Jonah said hopefully.

She glanced back. "My sweater?" she asked. "It's a purple rag, pinhead. I take it back: You're too daft to be a puppy. My sweater. You could have at least said my jeans."

"Is it too late?" Jonah asked.

"Yes."

Jonah smiled and hurried after her. He already felt a bit better. Maybe Sally was stuck. But Jonah wouldn't be. He would save Martin and the others and go back to the ISR. Then he'd figure out a new plan. One way or another, Jonah was going home.

"Hurry up, rat boy," Sally called. "Don't push your luck."

Jonah picked up his pace. He just had to make sure Sally didn't kill him first.

CHAPTER FOURTEEN

SALLY LED JONAH ALONG AT A BRISK PACE until the Haunted Passage came to a sudden halt at a set of big yellow-and-black steel doors. The faded words RESTRICTED: CREW MEMBERS ONLY were written across them in black letters.

"The Unknown Zone?" Jonah guessed.

Sally just nodded and punched 111 into the control panel. The big doors slid open.

"How'd you know—"

"Found the training manual," Sally said. "They're not very creative." She waved a hand over the hall. "Welcome to the Unknown Zone. Or, as I call it, Moaning Manor."

It was easy to see why she'd picked that name. The groaning of the ship's engine filled the hallway, as if the ghosts had gathered in the walls here. The hallway itself was made of the same gray metal as the rest of the ship, but it was shorter and wider, and faded yellow and black paint ran along the walls like a warning stripe. Moaning Manor was even scarier than the Haunted Passage, Jonah decided.

It was the perfect home for the Shrieker.

"Where does it live?" Jonah asked quietly.

Sally shrugged. "Who knows? There are service shafts and back hallways and other places where it probably crawls into. I don't think it knows how to use doors."

"Have you seen it?"

She laughed. "If I did, do you think I'd still be here? A word to the wise. Don't try. I've never seen it. But I've heard kids who have. I've heard them scream."

Jonah blanched. "Let's keep moving."

"Good idea."

She pointed out a few doors as they went. "That's the door I'd like to get into. I think it leads to the shuttle bay. Only way off this ship. But that code isn't 111. And they only go there for two reasons: to pick up new Space Raiders or drop them off in the Dark Zone."

Jonah made a mental note to inspect that control panel.

She pointed at a very wide gray steel door. "And here we have the storeroom. That's a 111. I suggest grabbing a few extra food bars—"

She suddenly stopped.

Jonah frowned. "What?"

For a moment, she didn't say anything. Then she turned to Jonah.

"They're coming," she said quickly. "Inside!"

She punched the code in, and she and Jonah ran inside the storeroom. Sally slapped the door panel, shutting the door behind them. The room was about five times the size of the cafeteria, and it was stacked high with big cardboard boxes labeled RATIONS.

"Get behind the stacks," Sally said. "Go!"

She and Jonah squeezed through the stacks of boxes and cowered down near the back of the room. Jonah had a narrow view of the door from his position.

"The Shrieker will come in here?" Jonah asked, confused. "I thought it can't use doors."

"Not the Shrieker," Sally murmured.

The storeroom door slid open, and two men walked inside. Jonah hadn't gotten a very good look at the two men who had taken Martin, but he knew these men were different. One had skin as black as space, a shaved head, and a thick, puckered scar running from his left eyebrow down to his chin. One of his eyes was missing. In its place was a circular metallic replacement with a red lens. He wore a holstered gun on his right hip.

The second man was a contrast in every way. His skin was pale, almost as pale as the commander's, and he had long straggly white hair and a beard that still had a few streaks of black. His skin was wrinkled and worn and slightly yellowed from age, and he was at least six inches shorter than the man beside him.

The only similarity was the gun.

The two men walked over to the boxes, and each grabbed one.

"I'm sick of these bloody rations," the older man snarled. "The captain is the cheapest guy I ever met. I don't believe we're running short on the real food. I think the captain wants to make sure he doesn't run short, so he's switching us over to the rations."

"We still have three weeks there and four back," the other man said. His voice was deep and intimidating. "We might even run out of the rations."

"So we take them from the kids," the older man said, wrapping his hands around the box and starting for the door. "Easy enough."

"If they don't make it, we don't get paid."

"How would they know?" the older man sneered. "We should fire Leppy out into space, if you ask me. Save some food. Not to mention the bloody shouter. If I catch that bugger, I'll burn 'im down on the spot."

"Good luck," the other man said. "Drop a box at the brig. Let them fight over it."

The door slid shut behind them, and Sally stood up again. "Pleasant bunch," she said. "You might want to avoid them, too. Especially Red Eye. He's a scary one. Wrinkles is mean, but he's also slow and doesn't hear too well. I wouldn't worry about him."

She walked over to an open box.

"Stuff your pockets, rat boy. We need to get going—"

"How did you know they were coming?" Jonah asked.

She shrugged. "I'm used to listening for footsteps. They echo in the walls."

She tossed him a food bar, and he shoved it in his pocket. None of it made sense to Jonah. Why did the crew have weapons and the Space Raiders didn't? Why were the Space Raiders not allowed to go anywhere on the ship, if they were heroes chosen to save the universe?

Sally must have seen him frowning. "Sometimes it's better not to ask," she said.

"No," Jonah said. "I want to know what's going on."

Sally shrugged and stuffed some food bars in her pockets. "Suit yourself. But you're on your own. There's only one place to go for answers, and you just saw who lives there. Time to go. If you really want to save your friends, you'll want to take the engine room. I'll show you the door—"

"Attention," a commanding, cruel-sounding voice boomed over the PA. "I have just been informed that the boy who attacked First Mate Grouter has gone on the run in my ship. The rules are being broken of late, and I'm tired of it. I know you can hear me, Jonah Hillcrest. Turn yourself in today, and I will lessen your punishment. Continue running and I will lock you up in a cell and throw away the key, if I don't decide to just throw you out the air lock first."

Jonah's eyes widened. He saw Sally staring at him in wonder.

"To everyone else on this ship—and I mean

everyone—if anyone helps the guilty party, they will be punished as well. And to my crew: Whoever captures the attacker and brings him to me wins double pay. Think fast, boy. The hunt is on."

The announcement finished, and Jonah just stood there, trying not to tremble. Things just kept getting worse. Now he had Red Eye hunting for him.

Sally smiled and shook her head. "You are one dead space rat."

CHAPTER FIFTEEN

JONAH TRIED TO MAKE SENSE OF THE announcement. Why did the captain think he had attacked First Mate Grouter? He didn't even know how to use his bonker. Had the ISR told the captain it was him? He certainly wouldn't put it past them. One thing was for sure: His mission to rescue Martin and the other Space Raiders was suddenly a whole lot more difficult.

Jonah waited for Sally to run off. After all, he was a wanted boy now, and the crew would be tirelessly scouring the ship to find him.

He had a feeling that double pay would inspire a lot of hunters.

But to his surprise, Sally didn't leave. She just stared at him with a lopsided smirk, shaking her head in disbelief.

"Shouldn't you be running away from me?" Jonah asked.

He was probably pushing his luck, since he certainly didn't want her to leave, but he had to ask. It occurred to him that a real hero would probably force her to run for her own safety, but in fairness, he had never claimed to be a hero.

She brushed her raven hair out of her eyes. "Run?" she asked. "No way. You're more interesting than I thought. I didn't know you'd attacked a crew member."

Jonah knew he should tell her he didn't actually attack First Mate Grouter, but she was suddenly looking at him like he was more than a space rat, so he decided to keep that to himself. Besides, he needed Sally Malik's help.

"Yeah," he said, trying to look tough, "I bonked him all right. Right on the knee. A real hard bonk. I also stole the List."

Sally frowned. "Why did you steal the List?"

Jonah shrugged. "Something to do."

Sally looked at him for a moment. She was probably trying to figure out how a skinny eleven-year-old had managed to accomplish such impressive feats. But maybe it was too dangerous to accuse a wanted crew bonker of lying, because she just smiled again.

"What was your Space Raider name?" she asked.

"Jonah the Now Incredible," he said.

She gestured at the door. "Well, Jonah the Now Incredible, where to now?"

He met her eyes. "The crew's quarters. I have Space Raiders to rescue."

"Did you just hear that announcement?" she asked incredulously. "The captain and his crew are currently hunting for you. And you want to go to their turf?"

Jonah shrugged again. "It's probably the last place they'd look for me."

Sally opened her mouth to retort and then paused. "That kind of makes sense. We'll take the service shafts from the engine room. Follow me."

She hurried over to the storeroom door and stuck her ear against the metal, listening for footsteps in the hallway. Satisfied, she pressed the door controls, and they crept into the corridor. Jonah was watching for a red eye in the shadows. Sally quickly led him across the hall and punched 111 into the engine-room control panel. The door slid open.

Jonah followed Sally inside and came to an abrupt halt.

He looked around in awe. The engine room was massive. It was four stories high and crisscrossed with hanging walkways and service ladders and conduits and power lines. The engine core itself was a massive cylinder of tarnished steel and black casing from which all the conduits and pathways led. Hundreds of blinking buttons covered its exterior, and other machinery—cooling towers and overflows and regulators—rose up like rock formations around it. Taken at once, the room looked like a huge spiderweb of black steel and multicolored power lines, with the engine itself being the great spider perched in the center of its work.

It was at once terrifying and impressive. It was also very loud.

The moaning, groaning sound of the engine bounced off every wall and echoed down service shafts and conduits, creating a reverberating, howling orchestra of noise.

"Cool, right?" Sally asked, raising her voice a little over the noise.

Jonah nodded.

"Of course," she continued, "it's also the home of the Shrieker, so let's move before it eats us."

She led him to a service ladder and started climbing up. Jonah followed very slowly. He'd never climbed a ladder before. It seemed a bit dangerous. When they reached the first walkway, which was about fifteen feet above the ground, Jonah climbed off the ladder and snuck a peek over the side. He wasn't overly good with heights, either. Even worse, the railings were mostly broken or bent or missing altogether.

Sally was already hurrying along, so he forced himself to get up and go after her. Each hanging walkway led to service shafts that disappeared into the bowels of the ship. There must have been eight or nine walkways stretching out from the engine, all leading to different service shafts and connected to each other by thick wires and steel beams.

"You come here often?" Jonah asked, glancing down again.

He wasn't looking forward to climbing higher into the spiderweb.

"Sometimes," she said, "but it's a little too exposed. I prefer the air ducts."

They reached the next ladder, and Sally climbed up like a monkey. She was clearly used to moving around in the web. Jonah reluctantly put his hands on the rungs, ready to follow her. Then he saw something in the corner of the room. It hadn't been visible when they first walked in, since it was on the other side of the engine core. But it was hard to miss now.

There, sitting in the corner, was a giant pile of bonkers.

Hundreds of them had been thrown onto the pile, while others lay scattered around it from where they'd rolled off. There were enough for an army of Space Raiders. He considered going down to get one, but he needed both hands to climb. Jonah wondered why they kept the bonkers here. It seemed like a strange place for weapons.

He slowly climbed up after Sally, his feet unsteadily finding the metal rungs below him. Sally peered down, looking impatient.

"You climb like a grandma," she said as he crawled onto the walkway.

"I think my grandma climbs better," Jonah muttered.

Sally raised an eyebrow, and Jonah remembered that he was supposed to be an orphan. He didn't want Sally Malik treating him like the other Space Raiders did.

"I mean, she probably did," Jonah said quickly. "Never met her. Where are you from?"

Sally frowned and then started for the next service ladder. "London. I told you."

"Right," Jonah said, hurrying after her. "Any siblings?"

Sally looked back. "A brother. John."

"And he—"

"Wasn't chosen," Sally said curtly, starting up a ladder. "They left him behind."

Jonah climbed after her. They were at least thirty feet off the floor, maybe more, and he was trying his best not to look down. The engine hummed even louder beside him.

"How old was he?"

She paused. "Seven," she said. "He was still in our foster home. I ran away."

"Why?"

She reached the top of the ladder and stood up. "Because I was a bad kid," she said, just loudly enough for him to hear it. "And he wasn't. And now I left him behind."

Jonah climbed onto the walkway. "You seem nice to me."

She laughed. "That's because you're a dimwit. You also thought I was a space princess." She helped him up. "What about you? Were you a runaway?"

Jonah hesitated. "Yeah. I lived in a forest."

"A forest?" she asked skeptically.

He nodded. "Yep. I stole clothes and food sometimes, when I wasn't living off of berries and nuts and rabbits."

"You ate rabbits?"

"Sometimes," he said.

He'd never even seen a wild rabbit. He hoped they still existed.

"It makes sense," she said thoughtfully, looking at his hair.

He patted it down, feeling a little self-conscious. "We should keep moving."

"Yeah," she said, giving him another once-over. "Any other secrets?"

"That's it," Jonah said.

She nodded and kept moving. "One last ladder. Then we head into the shaft."

By the time they reached the top walkway, Jonah was trembling, he was so scared. The floor looked far away below them, half visible through the spider web. There was no railing here, so he stayed right in the middle of the walkway as Sally led him away from the engine core and toward the outer walls. The walkway led straight into a dark service shaft lit only by a narrow band of lights running along the wall.

"This shaft leads to a staircase," Sally said. "And that staircase leads to the top level. The crew's quarters and the bridge. What we're going to do then I have no idea.

There might be some air ducts we can sneak into. I don't know. I've never been up there."

"We'll figure it out," Jonah said. "Just get me to the staircase and—"

He was cut off by a squeak. Jonah quickly turned around and saw something running toward him at a disturbingly fast pace. Large as a small cat, it was covered in dark brown fur and had a long, slender tail. Jonah had seen rats in pictures before, but they'd never looked this big. This was a super rat.

And it was coming right for him.

He didn't have time to react. The rat bounded over his feet, and Jonah yelped and jumped backward. That was a bad idea. He stepped right off the walkway and felt a terrifying sense of weightlessness as he started falling toward the distant engine-room floor.

CHAPTER SIXTEEN

JONAH REACHED OUT WILDLY, AND HIS FINGERS slid across the metal walkway and caught right at the edge. A powerful jolt ran through his body as his momentum suddenly stopped, and then he was just hanging there, his fingers still sliding toward the edge.

He felt his whole body straining. He didn't exactly have a lot of upper-body strength. Jonah looked down. He could see black-metal floor more than sixty feet below him, right through an opening in the spiderweb of conduits and power lines and walkways. If he fell, nothing would catch him.

"Jonah!" Sally said, grabbing on to his arms. "Hold on!"

"Okay," he managed weakly. His arms were already throbbing.

She struggled to get a firm grip. "You're going to have to pull yourself at the same time," she said, trying to position herself into a crouch. "You're too heavy."

Jonah saw his feet dangling below him. For a second, he felt faint.

He quickly fought it off.

"I'll try," he said.

His fingers started sliding toward the edge again. Jonah started to panic.

"Ready?" Sally asked urgently.

"Yeah," Jonah said.

"I don't know if this is going to work," she murmured.

"That's comforting," Jonah said.

"On three, I'm going to pull," she said. "You pull yourself up as well."

"Right," Jonah said. His fingers continued to slide. "Start counting."

"One . . . two . . . three!"

Sally lunged backward, pulling him with her, and Jonah heaved onto the walkway, trying to pull himself up. It barely worked. Sally slammed onto her back, still clutching Jonah's wrists, and his legs just cleared the edge of the walkway.

They lay there for a moment, locked in an embrace.

"Are you going to get off?" Sally asked.

"Yeah," Jonah said, rolling off of her. "Sorry. Thanks."

She slowly pushed herself to her feet. "No problem. Try not to fall again, though. That kind of hurt. What kind of forest are you from, anyway? It was just a rat."

"Took me by surprise," Jonah muttered. "Was that Whiskerface?"

She frowned. "Who?"

"Never mind," Jonah said. "Can we get off this walkway?"

"Good idea."

They hurried off and into the service shaft. Jonah was very happy to have walls and solid ground beneath him again. He decided he didn't like the engine room. He never liked spiders anyway.

The service shaft was about seven feet high and four feet across. A strip of yellow lights ran all along one wall, and there were red, green, and yellow power lines and steel-encased conduits running along the ceiling as well. The walls were also covered with removable panels and smaller tunnel entrances.

They walked by several junctions where one service shaft intersected another, and Jonah saw service ladders poking out of the floor in several locations.

"There are main shafts," Sally said quietly, "like this one, and also small ones and vertical ones and little areas you can crawl into. It's a maze within a maze."

"And the Shrieker lives in here?" Jonah asked nervously.

"I think so," Sally murmured. "It might have a room tucked away somewhere in the maze."

Jonah followed her through the service shaft, constantly listening for shrieks and laughter. He was just beginning to think the service shaft ran on forever when Sally stopped in front of a doorway. Inside was a black-metal staircase.

She glanced at him. “This leads into the crew’s quarters.”

Jonah nodded. “Thanks. I understand if you want to leave now—”

“Not yet,” she said, grinning. “This is just getting exciting. After you.”

Jonah started up the stairs. His footsteps echoed loudly in the close quarters of the narrow stairwell. They soon reached the top, where the staircase ended at a door with a small, grimy window built into it. Jonah peeked through.

The window looked out on another corridor much the same as Squirrel Street and the Haunted Passage. The only difference was that all the light panels worked here. He glanced up and down the hallway and finally spotted an air grate about twenty feet down.

“There,” he said, pointing it out to Sally.

“And what do we do when we’re in there?” she asked.

He paused. “I guess we’ll figure it out.”

“Good plan,” she muttered.

Jonah took one last look down the hallway. “All clear.”

He hit the door panel, and it slid open. Jonah snuck down the passage, sticking close to the rusted gray walls. He was ready to run back to the shaft at a moment’s notice.

Jonah reached the air grate without incident and bent down to pull it off.

"Look," Sally whispered.

He followed her gaze and saw an open door a little farther down the hall. The lights were on inside, and he saw a computer console and a table. They exchanged a look.

"Let's check it out," Jonah said.

He really wanted to get into the air duct and hide, but he also wanted answers. This looked like a good place to start. He hurried over to the open door, Sally close behind. Taking a quick look inside, he nodded and went in.

"Check the computer," he said.

The small room looked like a workstation. The shelves held a few old files and star maps, while a second desk and computer sat in the far corner.

"Needs a password," Sally said. "It's not 111, either."

Jonah wandered over to the other computer. He punched 111 into the home screen. Nothing. He was just turning back to Sally when he saw a brown folder on the desk. There was a label on the front with the typed words PROJECT WEED.

Jonah frowned and picked up the folder. He opened it to the first page and found a small star map of the known galaxy. He didn't see any areas labeled "Dark Zone," but there were some circled planets with numbers over them: one to eight. There were also scribbled notes on the page of travel-time estimates and little hand-drawn stars labeled *possible sighting*. Jonah flipped to the next page. It contained a picture of a planet called PER-1. Descriptions of the planet's physical characteristics were listed below it.

"What did you find?" Sally asked.

"I have no idea," Jonah said. "Have you ever heard of Project Weed?"

She shook her head. "Anything about the Space Raiders?"

"Not yet. Maybe—"

"Shh," Sally said suddenly.

They fell silent, and she looked at Jonah, her eyes wide.

"Footsteps."

Jonah looked around the room in a panic. The desk was the only place to hide.

"Here," he mouthed, and then quickly climbed behind the desk.

The desk was placed diagonally in the corner of the room, leaving a big-enough gap for them to fit between the desk and the wall. Sally was there in an instant, hunkering down beside him. She was just in time.

Jonah heard someone walk inside, muttering to himself.

"Get the folder, Bogg. Hurry up, Bogg. I need it right now, Bogg. I don't care if you're not on duty, Bogg. You're always on duty, Bogg."

The man was heading right for them. Jonah and Sally hunkered even lower.

"I need to see PER-7, Bogg," the man continued. His voice was raspy and rough.

Jonah heard him snatch the Project Weed file off the desk. He exchanged a confused look with Sally as the man started for the door.

"Whatever you want, captain," the man said. "I live to serve."

He left the room and started down the hallway, still muttering about the captain.

"That was close," Sally said.

"Too close," Jonah agreed. "We better get to the air duct."

She nodded, and they crept out from behind the desk and started for the door. Jonah was about to take a look into the hall when he heard voices. He quickly stepped against the wall, pulling Sally with him.

"Worst idea ever," Sally whispered.

The voices grew louder.

"Should save the bars, if you ask me," one man said. It sounded like Wrinkles.

"And starve 'em all?" another man asked. His voice was familiar too. It was the man who had taken Martin the Marvelous. "Be a nasty cleanup."

"Nah," Wrinkles said. "We throw 'em in the air lock and dispose. Easy. We do it with the garbage."

The other man chuckled. "And Leppy, too?"

"Him most of all," Wrinkles muttered. "Cost us two weeks."

"You got somewhere to be?"

"Yeah," Wrinkles said. "The bar. I'm taking a leave after this job. I'm sick of carrying these miserable kids across the galaxy. And now I have to feed the troublemakers on top of everything else. This is not what I signed up for. We should be back looting the transport ships like the old days."

"Dangerous game," the other man said.

"And a profitable one," Wrinkles said.

They were past Jonah and Sally now, and their voices were growing a bit fainter. Then they came to a stop. Jonah heard a door slide open.

"Here you go, you miserable buggers," Wrinkles said. "I must have forgotten a bar, so you can fight it out to see who goes hungry. I know my guess," he sneered.

The door slid shut, and the two men walked past Jonah and Sally again, talking and laughing about some transport ship they'd once hijacked. Jonah waited until their voices had faded away, and then he glanced at Sally.

"Space pirates," he murmured.

She nodded.

"Follow me," Jonah said. There was something he had to see.

He took a quick look out the door and then hurried down the hallway.

"What about the air duct?" Sally whispered behind him.

"I need to do something first."

He jogged down the hallway, looking from door to door. And then he saw it. One door had a square of solid glass built into it, and a well-lit room was visible inside. And there, scooping up the food bars, were the captured Space Raiders. Jonah didn't know how many had been taken overall, but there were a lot. He saw Martin and Samantha and nine others he didn't recognize, though two looked like the captured hall guards. He even saw one younger boy who looked a lot like Victoria. He'd found her brother too.

Jonah did notice that Alex wasn't in there. Jonah hoped he'd made it back to Sector Three.

There was a control panel next to the door. Sally tried 111 and shook her head.

"Didn't think so," she said.

Jonah was about to tap on the glass to let them know he was there when he saw the grizzled, sallow-faced man with bright red hair sitting in the corner. He guessed it was Leppy, the imprisoned crew member. And he knew Leppy would gladly give him up to get back into favor with the captain.

Leppy was just glancing toward the door when Jonah stepped out of the way.

"Let's get to the grate," he said quickly.

He and Sally jogged back to the air grate, pulled it off, and climbed inside. Not until it was firmly in place and they were tucked farther up the supply duct did Jonah finally relax a little.

He looked at Sally. "I need your help."

CHAPTER SEVENTEEN

JONAH AND SALLY DECIDED THE FIRST STEP to a successful rescue was information. They needed to find out more about the movements of the crew and the controls for the brig door panel, all without being detected by a group of bloodthirsty space pirates.

Jonah was starting to feel like a hero again. Just a really scared one.

They began by crawling through the entire air duct. Unfortunately, the section they were in ended before the brig itself; Sally guessed that the air in the brig was being fed in through a grate in the ceiling. They wouldn't be able to get in that way.

The air duct also ended before the thick double doors to the bridge, where the captain and his crew piloted the *Squirrel* across space. Jonah had hoped to spy on the bridge for a while and figure out exactly where they were going, but no luck there, either. However, the air duct did travel along the rest of the crew's quarters, with scattered grates staring out into the short hallway along the way, which Sally named Pirate Road.

Watching from those grates, Jonah and Sally managed to piece together a loose schedule for the crew. Over the course of three to four hours, Jonah saw five different pirates, including Red Eye, Wrinkles, Bogg, and the two pirates who had captured Martin—Sally had named them Weasel and Beardy. Sally told him she'd seen two others as well, including one she guessed was First Mate Grouter and a stout, foul-mouthed woman she called the Space Witch.

So that left them with seven pirates, Leppy, and Captain White Shark himself. Sally had never even seen him. She had just heard stories.

"Even the crew is afraid of him," she whispered as they sat hunched beside an air grate, waiting for crew members to walk by. "If you ever run into him, run."

"I just wish we could get onto the bridge," Jonah said. "I want to know where we're going."

Sally frowned. "We're going to the Dark Zone. Same as every other trip."

"Then what's PER-7?" Jonah asked.

"Who knows," she said. "A certain part of the Dark Zone, maybe? All I know is, Space Raiders go into the Dark Zone and they don't come back." She paused. "I hope that's because the fight is still going on and you're all just reinforcements."

Jonah glanced at her. "And not replacements."

She nodded.

Jonah pictured himself being dropped onto some haunted alien planet with a bonker and a bunch of marching, uniformed kids at his side. A thick purple haze lay over the planet, sweeping over scorched red soil and barren cliffs that rose to the sky. They walked between the cliffs, the commander at the lead, and then a bellowing cry rang through the air and clawed green monsters with black eyes streamed down the cliffs toward them. Jonah lifted his bonker, preparing to fight, and said a silent good-bye to his family, knowing he would never leave that planet.

Jonah turned back to the grate. "I don't think I want to go to the Dark Zone."

"I don't blame you," Sally muttered.

It occurred to Jonah that the thought of hiding in an air duct spying on pirates and plotting to rescue a group of Space Raiders might have once been just as crazy as marching across a red planet with a bonker. He tried to remember what he was like before. A quiet, shy kid with no friends. A scared little boy who watched other kids venture into the woods because he was too afraid of the trees and even more afraid of what the other kids would say if he tried. That was just a few short weeks ago.

Space was changing him.

Maybe it was the musty air or the gray walls or the haunting, moaning engine. Maybe it was the constant threat of exile and the Shrieker and the crew. But Jonah

Hillcrest was suddenly a boy who rescued prisoners. And he kind of liked that Jonah.

Now he just had to figure out how to do it.

He heard a door slide open with a whoosh. It seemed most of the doors worked in the crew's quarters, unlike in the rest of the ship. Sally said they had power-supply issues to much of the *Squirrel* but that the crew had managed to maintain the power lines to their own section. She'd seen them fusing a line together once in the engine room before she'd quickly scurried back into the safety of the shadows.

They were watching the hallways from the air duct when heavy footsteps suddenly approached the grate. Jonah leaned back just a little, being sure not to get his face too close to the light. As in the lower levels, the grates were mostly obscured by tight metal panels, but you could get a glimpse from certain angles. And so he bent to take a look just as she walked by holding a small pile of food bars.

Space Witch.

"Stout" was definitely the word for her. Her legs were as thick as tree trunks, and her faded brown pants strained and pulled with every step. Jonah bent down a bit lower and saw that she wore a white tank top with a black jacket, revealing a bit of a belly and bulging arms that were almost as thick as her legs. Her hair was a greasy mess of brown strands pulled back into a very tight bun.

Her face was flushed red and scarred and pulled into a ferocious scowl.

Jonah was still watching her when she suddenly slowed her pace. Her dark eyes flicked around the hallway. She knew she was being watched.

Jonah quickly pulled back, propping himself against the wall of the air duct. He waited, listening to the slow, scraping footsteps in the hall as the Space Witch looked around. If she pulled open the grate, they were finished. The seconds ticked by.

Finally, the Space Witch continued down the hall, and Jonah slumped in relief.

"Was it her?" Sally asked.

Jonah nodded. "And she really lives up to the name. Let's get back to the main duct. I don't want to be here when she comes back."

They crawled back into the main air duct and sat beside each other, bent awkwardly in the small space. It was time to come up with a plan.

"Have we learned anything?" Sally asked.

Jonah paused. "Well, we know how many there are. We think. A crew of nine, including the captain and Leppy. All with nasty-looking guns strapped to their hips."

"Yes, that's an important point," Sally said. She brushed her hair out of her eyes. "So we know who will be killing us if we get caught."

"Right," Jonah said.

"You sure you want to do this?"

He nodded. "We can't leave them in there. I owe Martin. And I told someone else I'd save her brother if I got the chance."

"Was it a girl?" Sally asked.

"Maybe."

She rolled her eyes. "Pretty?"

Jonah felt his cheeks flush. "I guess. I don't know. Didn't really think about it."

"Boys," she said, shaking her head. "You're all the same. One bat of the eyelashes and you'll take on a ship full of pirates." She batted her long black eyelashes at him. "Just don't forget about the space princess. I'm so very helpless."

"We should make a plan," Jonah said, trying to change the subject.

She smiled a toothy grin. "Fair enough, Jonah the Now Blushing. Any ideas?"

Jonah ignored her. "Well, they don't seem to feed the prisoners on a regular schedule. Not that it would matter if they did, because we don't have any way of telling time. We also don't know the password for the brig door, which is definitely a problem."

"This is great so far," Sally said.

"So even if we wait until they've just been fed and everyone seems to be either asleep or at their stations, we still have absolutely no way of opening the door and rescuing them. Unless we figure out the password."

"Or if we don't need a password," Sally said slowly.

Jonah glanced at her. "What?"

"Why do the doors automatically slide open here and not anywhere else?"

"Because they have power," Jonah said. "Oh."

Sally smiled. "Yeah."

"Do you remember where that power line was?"

"I think so," she said. "The rest of the *Squirrel* is in some sort of emergency-power mode. A few lights work, but no automatic doors and limited heat. I've heard them talk about it before. That's to conserve power. But if we knock out that power line leading to the crew's quarters, we should shut everything off. Lights, heat, and door controls."

Jonah nodded. "Then let's go turn off the lights."

"That's the one," Sally said, pointing at a green power line.

They'd followed the power line all through the service shafts and back to the engine room, and they stood there now on the highest walkway. The power line plunged directly into the core and was surrounded by a boxy steel casing that was within an arm's length of their walkway.

"How do you know?" Jonah asked, frowning.

She pointed at a ring of melted green rubber on the power line. "Because it was damaged before. I heard them arguing about the lights. It's definitely the one."

"All right," Jonah said. "Now we just need something sharp—"

Sally rolled her eyes. "You're going to cut a power line? Have you thought of what might happen to the person who cuts it?"

Jonah paused. "Right."

He looked around the room for inspiration, though that was pretty hard to do when looking down made him queasy. He shuffled to the edge of the walkway—after taking a quick look for super rats—and peered over the side. Then he saw it.

The giant pile of bonkers.

"There," he said.

Sally looked at him. "You want to hit it with a metal pole instead? I don't think you understand—"

"Not hit it," Jonah said. "Throw bonkers at it. If we get a direct hit, we might be able to knock that casing off. Or at least damage the wire."

Sally examined the casing skeptically. "It's possible."

"Do you have a better idea?"

She sighed. "Let's go get some bonkers."

It turned out to be a fairly difficult process. Eventually, Jonah ended up tucking his pants into his socks and filling the pant legs with bonkers, which allowed him to slowly climb back up again. Sally shook her head, but she did the same thing.

After a long, slow climb back to the top, Jonah yanked his pants out of his socks and started pulling out the bonkers. He'd managed to get four in each pant leg.

When the bonkers were out, he turned to the green wire.

"Do we aim for the wire or the casing?" he asked.

"I don't throw bonkers around very often," Sally muttered. "Try both."

Jonah nodded and picked up the first bonker. He had never been much of an athlete. Actually, he'd only ever played sports when he was forced to in gym class. And usually he was the last one picked. Well . . . always. He really should have participated.

He pulled the bonker back and threw it with all his strength. It missed by at least five feet. And he was only ten feet away from the wire. The bonker plummeted down the spiderweb and clanged loudly off the floor far below. Sally burst out laughing.

"That was the worst throw I've ever seen," she managed through her laughter.

Jonah grimaced and picked up another bonker. "It went pretty far."

"Yeah, downward," she said, wiping a tear from her eye. "Wow. That was good."

"It won't be when we alert the entire ship we're here," Jonah said. "You try."

Sally took a few steps forward. "You better join me, noodle arm."

Jonah rubbed his arm self-consciously and stepped beside her. "Let's see how good you are."

Sally immediately pulled back and threw a bonker. It hit the steel casing full on, denting the metal inward, and then the bonker flew right back toward them, whizzing past Jonah's head. He stood there for a moment, eyes wide, and then looked at Sally.

"Maybe try hitting the wire next," she said. "But that was right on."

"We were also closer," Jonah muttered.

He missed his next throw again and tried to ignore Sally's snort of derision. She threw two more, managing to hit the wire once, but it didn't have much effect. The bonkers kept clattering off the metal floor far below. Jonah knew the sound would echo down every service shaft on the *Squirrel*. They had to hurry.

He threw three more bonkers and managed to hit the engine core itself, the far wall, and nothing at all. It sounded like a clanging drum set in the engine room. Sally wasn't having much luck either. She hit the wire again and again, but it didn't break free of the engine. She threw her last bonker extra hard, but again, the wire didn't move. Jonah tried another bonker and missed completely. He only had two left.

"You must be a baseball player," she said.

He frowned at her. "Two left. You want one?"

"It's useless," she said, shaking her head. "The wire doesn't move."

"No," Jonah said thoughtfully, "but the casing did."

He walked closer to the steel casing—only a few feet away. The edge had dented right into the power line from where Sally had hit it and was pressing against the green exterior. If he hit it again in the same place, it might just pierce the line.

He glanced at Sally. "You might want to back up."

Sally raised her eyebrows. "You might want to back up too."

Jonah shook his head. "I'm not a baseball player. But I am a bonker."

He turned to the casing and raised the bonker over his head.

"I just have to let go at the last second."

Sally took a quick step back. "If you don't, you're going to fry like an egg."

"Thanks," Jonah murmured.

"Is she really worth it?" Sally asked. "I'll bat my eyelashes some more if you want."

"If I give up now, no one will rescue them," Jonah said tightly. "Besides, these pirates have taken enough Space Raiders. It's time to hit back."

With that, he swung the bonker directly at the steel casing. When it was about a foot from its mark, he let go. That was a good thing.

The bonker made clean contact with the casing, and the steel edge cut into the power line. Then it got very bright. A shower of white hot sparks burst out of the power line, and Jonah just managed to close his eyes as he fell backward onto the walkway. He heard Sally shouting in the background, but she was drowned out by the sizzling sparks.

Jonah hit the ground hard just as the shower of sparks ended, and he cautiously opened his eyes to see the last few sparks shoot out of the power line and disappear.

"That was unexpected," Jonah said. He felt a bunch of small burns on his face.

Sally bent over him. "Are you alive?"

"I think so," he said. "Did it work?"

Sally shrugged. "Well, that wire is certainly busted, so I'm guessing our pirate friends are currently sitting in the dark. Your fellow Space Raiders, too."

"Perfect," Jonah murmured.

She grinned. "You're full of surprises, Jonah the Now Incredible. Every time I think you've reached your stupidest moment, you manage to top yourself. It's very impressive. Now we better go hide in the service shafts until the crew comes. It's time to save your friends. Or get shot by a space pirate. Either/or."

She pulled Jonah to his feet, and he gingerly touched his face. It was stinging.

"I hope that was the hard part," Jonah muttered. "But I doubt it."

He was right. After hiding in a tiny side shaft until four grumbling, very unhappy crew members traipsed down the main shaft, shining a portable light along the power lines to check for damage, Jonah and Sally climbed out and ran toward the crew's quarters. The dim yellow lighting of the service shaft was still working, but it did little to push back the shadows.

Jonah had been very happy to catch a glimpse of a red eye in the darkness and to hear the brusque, husky voice of the Space Witch. At least they wouldn't run into them.

When they reached the quarters, he was relieved to see that Pirate Road was completely dark. He was just thinking they'd come up with the perfect plan when he looked down the hall toward the brig. There, guarding the door with a portable light each, were two crew members.

"Wrinkles and Weasel," Sally muttered. "Now what?"

"I don't know," Jonah said.

She glanced at him. "Think you can bonk them?"

"Two of them?" Jonah said. "They'll just shoot me."

"Yeah, probably," Sally murmured.

They stood there for a moment. Jonah had no idea what to do. All that, and they were stuck here. And they didn't have much time. Once Red Eye and the others fused the power line and restored power, they'd come right back here.

And Jonah and Sally had to be long gone when they did.

"I guess that's it—"

"We need a distraction," Sally cut in.

"I can try throwing my bonker down the hall," Jonah suggested.

"Yeah, that will work for one second," Sally said. She took a little pink hair tie out of her pocket and started pulling her long black hair into a ponytail. "I'll do it."

"You don't have to—"

"I've hid on this ship for long enough now," she said. "I want to hit back too."

Jonah smiled. "What are you going to do?"

"There's a main staircase that leads back down the ship," she said. "It's at the other end of Pirate Road. I'm going to shriek and run for the stairs. At least one of them will chase me. Probably both."

She stuck her hand out. Jonah looked at it, confused.

"Shake it, dimwit," she said.

He did as he was told.

"If we don't make it, it was a pleasure," she continued. "You're not the brightest Space Raider I've ever seen, but you might just be the bravest. Good luck."

"Meet you at the grate in the Haunted Passage?" Jonah said.

She smiled. "Deal. Now if you'll excuse me, I have to turn into a monster."

With that, she threw open the door, stepped into the hallway, and let loose a remarkably good impersonation of the Shrieker. It was so good that Jonah almost turned and ran down the stairs himself, and she was standing right in front of him.

It clearly had the desired effect.

He heard Wrinkles and Weasel shout and curse, followed by loud, clomping footsteps as they ran down the hallway. Sally took a quick look back, barely visible in the darkness, and then took off down the hall, laughing and cackling all the way.

Jonah quickly stepped to the side of the door as the two men ran by, and then he bolted down Pirate Road toward the brig. He looked back and saw Wrinkles and Weasel turn down the staircase, chasing the shrieking, cackling Sally. The plan had worked.

Jonah reached the brig and slid the door open. It was pitch black inside.

"Martin?" he asked, stepping into the room. "Samantha?"

"Jonah?" a familiar voice asked, sounding amazed. He heard shuffling and felt Martin's small hand on his arm. "What are you doing here?"

"Rescuing you," Jonah said. "You've done enough hard time."

He heard astounded whispers around the room.

Martin laughed. "I knew you were incredible, but this takes the cake. How did you turn off the power?"

"Long story," Jonah said. "Now, everyone, wherever you are, we need to go. The pirates are going to be back soon—"

The words were barely out of his mouth when a glaring light washed over the doorway. Weasel walked in right behind it, holding his portable light up like a lantern.

"Well, well, well," he said, a cruel grin spreading over his face, "looks like we caught a rat."

CHAPTER EIGHTEEN

WEASEL STEPPED THROUGH THE DOORWAY, his portable light washing over the brig. Jonah blinked against the white glare and saw the other prisoners blocking their eyes with their arms.

Jonah was frozen to the spot, the bonker hanging loosely in his hands. A million thoughts ran through his head. He tried to think of a way to escape, but there was none.

He was trapped.

"Wrinkles ran off," Weasel said, his dark, beady eyes fixed on Jonah, "but I thought, wait a second. The lights go out and then the Shouter comes to the crew's quarters for the first time ever?" He smiled, revealing yellow and black teeth. "That would have to be some coincidence. Then I think maybe someone put those lights out. Maybe someone wanted to get us away from the brig. Maybe some little rat is trying to save his friends."

His thin, calloused hand was resting on his gun. The other Space Raiders all just stood there with pensive looks, eyes darting to Jonah. All but one.

As Weasel stared at Jonah with that evil grin, Martin

the Marvelous was slowly edging along the wall. Jonah didn't know what he was doing, but he had to buy him time.

"You got me," Jonah said, his voice sounding a bit tinny. He tried to stand up a little straighter. "I'd like you to release my friends now."

Weasel stared at him for a moment and then burst out laughing. "This one's a comedian," he said, looking at Leppy. "You never told me how funny they were."

Leppy spared a dark look at him through his ratty black hair.

Weasel turned back to Jonah. "This batch is getting a little too courageous for my liking. Don't know what it is. We've locked you up. We've threatened you. Not sure what else we can do. Can't have you wandering around the ship, you know. Against the rules."

Martin was past Weasel now, still sliding along the wall. Jonah wondered if he was planning to run for it and tell the others. At least someone would get away.

He kept his eyes on Weasel. "I guess we're special," he said. "We're not afraid of a bunch of smelly pirates."

The other Space Raiders looked at him in amazement. Jonah instantly knew he'd crossed a line. Weasel narrowed his eyes.

"Is that so?" he asked quietly, looking around the room. "Is that what you think?"

Leppy was still watching from the corner.

Weasel took another step toward Jonah. "No one knows you're here, little boy," he said. "And no one cares. You know what I think? I think we need to make an example of you. Locking you in the brig wouldn't work. Didn't work before. No. Someone needs to die."

His slender fingers were hovering over his gun. Jonah felt his skin go cold. His hands started trembling. Martin was almost at the door now. He could take off and run. Weasel would have to let him go. But Martin the Marvelous wasn't running.

He started creeping back toward Weasel. He moved as quietly as a mouse, his socked feet padding off the metal floors with tiny, tiptoeing steps.

Weasel smiled even wider. "I think the captain would agree this once. But I won't ask, just in case. Any last words, hero?"

Jonah wanted to cry. He wanted to drop into a quivering ball and beg for his life and cry out for his parents and ask for mercy. But once again, space had changed him.

He just stared up at Weasel. The bonker was shaking. His knees were wobbling. He couldn't even bring himself to speak. But he didn't cry. He just faced his enemy bravely.

"I do," Martin said. "Good night."

With incredibly deft hands, Martin plucked the gun out of Weasel's holster, stepped back, and shot the space pirate in the chest just as he turned around. There was a flash of brilliant blue, and then Weasel fell face-first onto the floor.

The brig was completely silent. Leppy watched with wide eyes.

"Did you kill him?" Samantha asked.

Martin shook his head. "They keep their guns set on stun. Captain's orders. I heard them talk about it when they carried me up here." He smiled. "But he won't feel very good when he wakes up."

"We better move," Jonah said, scooping up the portable light. "Thanks, Martin."

"Least I could do," Martin replied. He turned the gun around and handed it to Jonah. "Here. The hero takes the gun."

Jonah smiled. "Then I guess you better hold on to it. Follow me."

He started for the door, his hands still shaking.

"How do we get back, Jonah?" Samantha asked.

"I know a secret way," he said. "Just stay close and—"

Leppy looked at him, his dark eyes barely visible through his hair. "What did you say your name was?" he asked softly.

Jonah glanced at him. "Jonah."

Leppy brushed the hair out of his eyes. "Jonah what?"

He hesitated. "Jonah Hillcrest."

Leppy stared at him for a moment and then burst out

laughing. It was a manic, uncontrollable laugh. His whole body shook and convulsed, and he grabbed his stomach and kept laughing like he'd gone completely mad. Jonah looked at Martin, confused.

"I'm dead," Leppy managed through his laughter. "I'm so dead."

"He's crazy," Samantha said. "Let's go."

Jonah nodded and led them out the door, unnerved by Leppy's reaction. The insane laughter followed them all the way down Pirate Road until Jonah plunged into the service shaft, the twelve freed Space Raiders close on his tail. He flicked the portable light off when he was through the door and put it down. They were safer in the shadows.

Jonah jogged down the staircase, peeked out the service shaft, and hurried out. Then he froze. He'd come to the crew's quarters through the engine room. He couldn't go back there.

Samantha stepped up beside him. "Where are we?"

"The service shafts," Jonah said. "But we can't go back the way I came. The pirates are down there fixing the power line. We need to find another way back."

"Have you seen the Shrieker?" Martin asked nervously.

"I've heard it," Jonah said. "It lives in here. Let's go the other way. Look for ladders and stairs. We just need to get down."

The group took in off in the opposite direction from

the engine room, Jonah at the lead. He wondered if Sally Malik was all right. He really hoped so.

"There," someone said, pointing at a service ladder that descended through the floor.

Jonah tucked the bonker into his belt and started down the ladder. He took a nervous look below him as he unsteadily felt for the rungs. If the Shrieker attacked now, he was finished. But there were no shrieks or laughs as he dropped to the service-shaft floor, and he pulled out his bonker and waited as the others climbed down with him.

"Two more floors," Jonah said. "Come on!"

They ran along the shaft until they found another ladder and repeated the same process. Jonah almost slipped on the way down. He really hated climbing.

The group kept moving in perfect silence, no one daring to speak in the heavy quiet of the service shafts. Samantha ran right beside him, looking far calmer than he felt. He could see why she was the most important adventurer. She was fearless.

They found the last ladder to the bottommost level. Jonah had just put his foot on the first rung when they heard it. A piercing, inhuman shriek echoed down the shaft.

Jonah glanced up at the others. "Move!" he shouted.

He climbed down the ladder as fast as he could and dropped to the floor. He looked around, raising the bonker.

But he realized the laughter was coming from the second level. Right where the others were waiting to use the ladder.

"Faster!" he said.

Samantha dropped down beside him, brushing the long hair out of her eyes and glancing at Jonah. "They're not going to make it."

"They'll make it," Jonah said.

More Space Raiders scurried down the ladder. The laughter was growing louder and louder. Eight of them were down when Jonah realized Martin was still up there. The shrieks were close now. The ninth Space Raider had just put her foot on the stairs when a shot rang out. A blue flash lit up the darkness above them, and the shrieking stopped. The ninth Space Raider dropped to the ground, and then Martin climbed down after them.

He grinned and patted the gun tucked in his belt. "I like this thing."

"Did you shoot it?" Jonah asked incredulously.

"No, just a warning shot. But it took off."

Jonah just shook his head. "Let's get you guys home."

It took a few minutes to locate in the eerie lighting, but they eventually found a door out of the service shaft. Jonah pulled it open and was greeted by the welcome sight of the Haunted Passage. He quickly looked around for Sally. The hallway was empty.

The rest of the Space Raiders hurried out. Jonah felt

his stomach knotting up. Had something happened to Sally?

"Shouldn't we keep moving?" Samantha asked.

"You guys go," Jonah said. "I have to go back for—"

"The space princess?"

Jonah turned and saw Sally walk out of the service shaft wearing a sly smile.

"I'm touched," she said. "But I'm fine. Wrinkles never had a chance."

Jonah heard the others whispering behind him, and he turned to face them. "This is Sally Malik, space rat. She's the one who helped me rescue you."

"I thought I was a space princess," she said, raising an eyebrow.

"Nah," Jonah said. "A princess couldn't shriek like that. Why don't you come back with us? You can live in the sectors again."

The smile disappeared from Sally's face. "I don't belong there. Sorry. And I don't think you lot belong there either." She glanced down the hall. "Speaking of which, time to disappear." She gave Jonah a mock salute. "See you in the wild."

With that, she took off down the hall like a flitting shadow, heading back to the Unknown Zone.

"Where did she come from?" Martin asked.

"Long story," Jonah said.

He started for Sector Three. The others fell into step

behind him. After everywhere else Jonah had been, the Haunted Passage almost felt like home.

He turned the corner into Death Alley, and the two guards instantly lifted their bonkers. Their eyes widened.

The first guard turned to her partner. "You better get the lieutenant."

CHAPTER NINETEEN

SECTOR THREE FELL INTO COMPLETE SILENCE when Jonah and the other Space Raiders walked down Squirrel Street with a still-shocked Lieutenant Gordon.

The lieutenant had come running down the hall with the guard, and when he'd turned down Death Alley, he looked like he'd seen a ghost. It took him a moment, but then he managed to compose himself enough to formally welcome them all back.

"The commander will want to see you immediately," he said. "Follow me."

Ben was the first Space Raider to see them in the hallway. He just stopped in his tracks, his mouth opening in disbelief, his eyes directly on Jonah. Everyone else did the same thing. They ran out of doorways, hearing the rumors, and then stopped and stared.

Even Willona and Jemma had no words. Willona just shook her head in amazement, smiling from ear to ear. Then came the reunions.

The first was Alex the Adventurer, who stepped out of

his room and saw his older sister. They might have been professional competitors, but they were siblings now. He broke into a wild smile, and his sister hurried over and gave him a hug. Samantha stepped back and messed up his hair and hugged him again.

"How—," Alex started.

Samantha nodded at Jonah. Alex looked at him, his cheeks bright red. He seemed almost ashamed, though Jonah couldn't imagine why.

"You're back!" Jonah said. "What happened?"

"Long story," Alex muttered. He patted Jonah on the arm. "Thank you."

Jonah just smiled. The next one was even better.

Victoria came running out of her room, saw her brother, and literally screamed in excitement and joy. She sprinted down Squirrel Street, right past Jonah and the others, and wrapped her little brother in a tight hug, tears streaming down her cheeks.

"Are you okay?" she said, grabbing his face with her hands and turning him both ways. "Did they hurt you?"

He shook his head, his eyes welling with tears as well. She hugged him again and looked like she might never let go. She was shaking with sobs now. Finally, she let him go, wiped his cheeks, and turned to Jonah. Before he could say anything, she walked over to him, grabbed his cheeks, and kissed him firmly on the mouth.

It was only for a second or two, but it felt longer to

Jonah. He'd never kissed anyone before. It was a bit strange with their lips mashed together like that, and he didn`t know if he was supposed to do anything, but he could see the appeal. Especially with Victoria, who opened her pretty eyes for just a moment before she let go.

He felt his cheeks burning as she stepped back and looked coyly at the floor.

"Thanks," she murmured. Then she turned to her brother, who looked more surprised than anyone. "Come on, Matty," she said. "We need to catch up."

She took him by the arm and led him to the cafeteria, sparing one last red-faced glance at Jonah before she hurried inside.

"Did she just kiss my spy?" Willona said to Jemma.

That comment broke the silence. Everyone started laughing and talking and hugging the freed Space Raiders from Sector Three. Martin and the two captured guards were swarmed by Space Raiders, while the ones from the other sectors watched with big grins. For a second, they were all kids. They were all happy.

But rules were rules. And there were important discussions to be had.

"Order!" Lieutenant Gordon said loudly, though even he had cracked a smile. "We're on our way to see the commander. Follow me." He paused. "Matt the Amazing can stay with his sister."

He continued down Squirrel Street, and Jonah and the others marched after him while the rest of the Space Raiders saluted and laughed and waved good-bye.

It was the same in Sector Two. The Space Raiders greeted their lost companions with hugs and cheers, and Lieutenant Potts watched in stunned disbelief as Jonah walked by, his pudgy round cheeks flushed red. Lieutenant Gordon slid open the thick double doors to Sector One, and Samantha was greeted with the loudest cheers yet.

It was the happiest walk of Jonah's life.

Finally, they reached the commander's headquarters, and Erna the Strong watched them approach in obvious confusion.

Jonah smiled. "Hi, Erna."

She just stared at him.

"Erna the Strong," Lieutenant Gordon said, "we need an immediate audience with the commander. Tell her . . . well, you know what to tell her."

Erna had just turned to open the door when it slid open. The commander, who so rarely showed emotion, looked visibly upset. Her dark, serious eyes were wide open.

"What did you do?" she whispered.

The meeting was called immediately. The lieutenants and Samantha and the other important Space Raiders sat down at their long tables while Jonah and the other rescued Space Raiders stood in front of them. Erna the Strong guarded the door as always.

But this time the hall in front of the door was packed with Space Raiders. Jonah could hear them whispering through the door. They all wanted to know what had happened.

The commander had quickly recovered after her initial reaction. There had been a lot of surprised looks and murmurs after what she'd said to Jonah, but she had taken control back. She'd warmly welcomed Samantha and the others and ushered them inside while calling for order from the other Space Raiders.

But she'd still given Jonah a dark look as he walked by.

Now she was sitting at the head table, eyes serious again, her cascading lightning-streaked hair falling over her shoulders, her finger tapping on the metal.

"What happened?" she asked.

Jonah explained everything. He saw her frown when he spoke of Sally Malik and Home Sweet Home and his journey into the Unknown Zone. He told them about his climb up the engine room, the super rat and near fall, Project Weed, the plan to rescue the others, and smashing the power line with the bonker. He told her about Martin saving them and Leppy laughing and their narrow escape through the service shaft.

She listened to everything very quietly, as did the others.

When he finished, she was silent for a moment. "I don't know what to do with you, Jonah Hillcrest," she said.

Samantha looked at her, frowning.

The commander met his eyes. "You've put us all in danger. The greatest danger the Incredible Space Raiders have ever faced on this ship. There's a war now, that's for sure. Captain White Shark will come for us. All of us."

There were a few murmurs from the rescued Space Raiders.

The commander clearly noticed. "But you have also saved our missing Space Raiders," she said. "Who we thought were gone. That makes you a hero." She tapped her fingernail on the table. "However, if we give you up, they may leave us alone."

Lieutenant Potts nodded. "It's the only way."

"Is that how we treat our heroes?" Samantha asked coolly.

"They'll want all the prisoners back with him," Lieutenant Gordon said.

Lieutenant Potts turned to him. "If that's what we have to do."

Now the murmurs from the rescued Space Raiders sounded rebellious. The commander's eyes flicked around the room. Erna the Strong was shifting by the door, clearly ready for action. But even she must have seen the gun tucked in Martin's belt. If Martin decided to fight, there was nothing she could do. The power had shifted to Jonah and the rescued prisoners.

He decided to use it.

"There's another way," he said, and everyone turned to him.

"What's that?" the commander asked.

"We leave the sectors."

Lieutenant Potts snorted. "That's insane. We'll all be eaten by the Shrieker. No one survives in the Wild Zones."

"He did," Samantha said.

Jonah nodded. "And so does Sally Malik. This is a big ship. We can all split up and hide until we reach the Dark Zone. They won't find us if we're careful. We know the crew is coming here. We know they want revenge. We have to leave."

He could see the lieutenants were afraid. Even Lieutenant Gordon. They had their rules and order and structure in the sectors. If they left, that was all gone.

The commander just tapped the table. Her eyes were fixed firmly on Jonah, and she seemed to be struggling to make a decision. Finally, she pushed her chair back and stood up. The other seated Space Raiders quickly followed suit.

She looked at her lieutenants. "Go back to your sectors," she said quietly, and her eyes shifted back to Jonah. "Tell everyone to pack their supplies. We're leaving."

CHAPTER TWENTY

JONAH SAT ALONE IN HIS ROOM, STARING out at the stars. He'd been sent to pack his belongings, but since he really only had his journal and a blanket, there wasn't much to pack. The rest of the Space Raiders were scurrying around Squirrel Street, packing food bars and bonkers and maps. He knew the same scene was playing out in all four sectors.

The Space Raiders had taken the news in stunned silence, which was broken only by a sharp command from Lieutenant Gordon. But as Jonah walked back to his room, he saw the fear in their faces. The sadness. They'd made a home here, and now they were being forced to abandon it. Willona had looked completely devastated.

Jonah didn't know what to think. Every time he did something, he managed to hurt the other Space Raiders. But he'd had to save the others. Hadn't he?

There was something wrong about all this. He knew that. But without any answers, he was just as lost as the rest of them. And that was a scary thing.

He pulled out his journal.

Dear Mom and Dad and Mara,

I'm back in Sector Three. I managed to survive the Wild Zones, barely, and rescue the captured Space Raiders. It was probably the bravest thing I've ever done. I thought that would just make me brave for good. But it didn't. I think I'm more scared than ever.

I don't know if you guys gave me up . . . if I was bad and you signed me up for this mission to save the universe to get rid of me. I like to think that you didn't. But if you did, I understand. I never said thank you. I mean, I did when you gave me gifts or a ride or passed me the potatoes, but not in general. Not for having me and raising me and giving me a home. I should have said thank you. Because now that I don't have one, I know that we all need a home. Even if we're not there all the time. We need somewhere we belong.

I still think of you guys as home. But the other Space Raiders, they don't have a real home. This is their home, and now they have to give it up too. They have it worse. So I'm going to keep pretending to be brave, because at least I have a home somewhere.

This might be my last entry. I'm bringing my journal, but we're heading into the Wild Zones. We might not survive. If that's the case, I wanted to say thank you. Thank you for giving me a home. I think I understand what that's worth now.

Sincerely,
Jonah the Now Incredible

He read over the note, and only then did he realize he'd signed it Jonah the Now Incredible. That brought a smile to his face.

Maybe he was starting to feel incredible after all.

He closed the journal and placed it inside his ratty old blanket. Folding it up, he prepared to take the bundle and head out to join the others.

But before he stood up, there was a knock at the door. He hurried over and slid it open. It was Victoria.

"Hi," she said shyly. Her hands fidgeted nervously at her stomach, while her dark eyes darted from his to the floor. "Can I come in?"

"Of course," Jonah said quickly, feeling his cheeks burning. He stepped back to let her in. "How's your brother?"

"Much better," she said, smiling. "He's already talking about your escape through the ship. He loves adventures. That's how he got caught in the first place."

Victoria walked over to the window and put her hands on the glass.

"You did get the best view, you know," she said, glancing back at him.

"I guess," Jonah replied. "It seems to make me sad more than anything."

She turned back to the stars. "Because you miss your parents?"

"Yeah," Jonah murmured.

"My parents died when I was seven," she said quietly, still facing the window. "Transport crash. They were heading back to Earth for a vacation. Left us with a nanny, but there wasn't enough to pay her when they were gone. We had grandparents on Earth, but they couldn't afford to fly us back across the solar system. So we got put in an orphanage. Matty and me. Lined up for foster care a few times, but we were never picked. We wouldn't split up, and no one wanted two kids. Not out on Triton. It's an expensive place. Every time they tried to make us split up, we ran away. Once we even stole protective suits and hid on the surface for three days. We were bad kids, I guess. The last time they tried, we ran away again. They let us stay out there. Use the shelter. We were there, living on the streets and begging, when they took us. Matty was asleep, but not me. I saw the two men right before they zapped us. Then we woke up here."

Victoria turned to face him.

"We liked it here. But when they took Matty . . . " Her voice faltered. "They took the last thing I had. That's why

I changed my name to the Avenger. That's all I wanted."

There were tears in her eyes now.

"But I didn't go after him. I didn't know how. I didn't know where to go."

She walked over to him and took his hand.

"I guess I'm just trying to say thank you. Again. You gave me back the only thing I have." She smiled. "Whatever happens, I'm on your side, Jonah the Now Incredible."

Jonah just stood there thinking that the hand she was holding was a bit clammy and was he sweating again and was she going to kiss him and did he have to do it better this time? They met eyes. It was official. She was going to kiss him again.

She started leaning in.

"Am I interrupting something?" someone asked from the door.

Jonah whirled around. Willona was standing there with her hands on her hips, scowling at Victoria. Victoria quickly dropped Jonah's hand.

"No," she said. "Just leaving."

She gave Jonah a final smile and hurried out of the room.

Willona turned her scowl to Jonah. "I'm supposed to come fetch you."

"For what?" Jonah asked.

"I don't know," she said curtly. "Lieutenant Gordon wants to see you." She paused. "So, are you two dating now?"

"Dating?" Jonah asked incredulously. "We're on a ship."

"It's an expression," she said, glaring at him. "Are you together?"

Jonah frowned. "I don't think so."

"You two were alone in your room," Willona pointed out, folding her arms.

"You're always in my room," Jonah said.

"Exactly," Willona replied, pointedly looking away. "I thought I was the only one."

"I'm confused," Jonah said.

She turned back to him. "Me too," she said. With that, she turned and marched down the hallway. "Now hurry up. A little move doesn't change anything. I have a career to think about. That's it, apparently. Just career for Willona the Awesome. Anything else just gets you hurt. Space is no place for crushes. Especially on spies."

Jonah just shook his head and followed her.

"Come in," Lieutenant Gordon said, and Jonah walked into his office.

He was sitting at his desk, surrounded by Ben the Brilliant and Ria the Smart, a short girl with pigtails and shrewd brown eyes. Willona had once told him that she was the smartest Space Raider on the ship, other than the commander. They all watched him enter.

"We've been making plans," Lieutenant Gordon said. "The Space Raiders are still being broken up into four sectors, of course, and we must each find a temporary home. We can split up even further, if need be. But we can't decide where to go. Ria the Smart pointed out that no Space Raider knows this ship better than you."

Ria nodded. Ben looked venomous.

Lieutenant Gordon slid the map toward him. "What do you think?"

Jonah approached the desk and looked over the map.

"Where are the others going?" he asked.

"Sector One is going up a level. The commander thinks they can hide in the service shafts there. Sector Two is doing the same thing on the third level. I don't know about Sector Four, but they may just stay in the service shafts here. Which leaves us with the fourth level, right below the crew's quarters."

Jonah shook his head. "That's too close. What about the Shrieker?"

"We have to take our chances," Lieutenant Gordon said, sounding a bit nervous.

Jonah looked at the map. In particular he looked at the big blank area labeled the Unknown Zone. He knew a lot of that area was the massive engine room. There was also the storeroom and the shuttle bay. But Sally had mentioned something else.

The Bubble. It had to be in there as well.

"I think I know a place," Jonah said. "We should head toward the Unknown Zone."

Ben snorted. "Great idea. Let's go to the most dangerous part of the *Squirrel.*"

"I made it out," Jonah said. "And they won't look for us there."

"Why?" Lieutenant Gordon asked.

"Because there's a locked door with a password," Jonah said. "Which I know."

Ria smiled. "Perfect."

Lieutenant Gordon met Jonah's eyes and then nodded. "It's decided, then. We'll head to the Unknown Zone. I grant you temporary leadership, Jonah the Now Incredible. I'm still in charge, but in the Wild Zones, you lead the way. You give the orders."

Ben looked at him in disbelief.

"Thank you, lieutenant," Jonah said, giving him a sharp salute. He was getting better at it now. "We should leave right away. The crew will find Weasel soon."

Lieutenant Gordon stood up. "Agreed. Gather Sector Three. It's time to move out."

The Space Raiders of Sector Three gathered in Death Alley, all holding sheets and blankets bundled with their few possessions in one hand and their bonkers in the other. They looked grim but determined.

They were Space Raiders, and they would complete their mission.

Jonah watched as Willona and Jemma talked near the

back in quiet voices, and as Victoria stood close to her brother. He watched as Alex stood with his chest swelled and his bonker in hand, ready to venture back into the wild. He watched as Martin gave him a lopsided grin, his bundle almost as big as he was.

The commander had confiscated the gun for her use after their meeting, so he was unarmed again. But Jonah knew there was more to Martin than met the eye.

He was glad to have him on his team.

Jonah was standing next to Lieutenant Gordon, who was taking a quick head count. When he was satisfied, he looked out over the assembled Space Raiders.

"I now pass over temporary leadership to Jonah the Now Incredible, who will lead us to the Unknown Zone and a safe hiding place. Listen to his orders in the Wild Zones." He paused. "I know we didn't want to leave our sector. But we all knew we had to do it eventually. In two weeks, we'll be at the Dark Zone. We just have to make it until then."

Daniel the Ninja, one of the rescued guards, put his hand up.

"Yes?" Lieutenant Gordon said.

"Is there going to be a bathroom there?" he asked.

Lieutenant Gordon looked at Jonah.

"Uh, I don't know," Jonah said. "I'm sure we'll find one."

"Maybe I should go before we leave," he said thoughtfully.

Lieutenant Gordon sighed. "I'm sure there will be a bathroom. Anyone else?"

Eric the Excellent put his hand up. "What if Jonah leads us to Captain White Shark?"

"He's not a spy, birdbrain," Willona said. "Just a heartbreaker."

"What's that?" Lieutenant Gordon asked.

"Nothing," she muttered.

Lieutenant Gordon frowned. "Okay, then. Is that it?"

A young girl put her hand up. "Are we ever coming back?" she asked softly.

Lieutenant Gordon hesitated. "Probably not. So say your good-byes."

That put a somber mood over the group again, and there were no more questions. Some looked back at Squirrel Street with sorrowful expressions. Others even whispered good-bye.

Daniel the Ninja patted the wall. "Good-bye, Death Alley," he said quietly.

Lieutenant Gordon nodded at Jonah.

"All right, everyone," Jonah said, trying to sound as commanding as he could. "Follow me. We'll move fast and silent. Ben, can you be the lead scout?"

Ben looked at him in surprise. "Yeah," he said awkwardly. "Sure."

"Good. Alex the Adventurer, you guard the rear. You're the weapons master."

Alex smiled and nodded.

"Let's move," Jonah said.

With that, he turned and started down the Haunted Passage. This time he wasn't following Alex or sneaking with Martin or running from a jailbreak. He was leading the Space Raiders, bonker in hand.

He wondered what was next.

He was still wondering that when the door next to him slid open. Wrinkles stepped out of the service shaft, his gun pointed directly at Jonah. He smiled cruelly.

"Drop your weapon, rat. It's time to meet the captain."

CHAPTER TWENTY-ONE

IT WAS BEN THE BRILLIANT WHO REACTED FIRST. He was just a step or two behind Jonah—not quite doing his job as lead scout—and completely ignored by the grizzled old space pirate, who was aiming only for his precious double pay.

That was a mistake.

Ben shouted some sort of war cry and swung his bonker with surprising force, knocking the gun clean out of a very surprised Wrinkles's hands. The gun went clattering down the Haunted Passage, and Wrinkles turned to Ben in shock.

"You miserable—," he growled, reaching out with his weathered old hands.

But the full might of the Space Raiders was upon him now. Lieutenant Gordon shouted, "Space Raiders . . . attack!" and the battle was on. Lieutenant Gordon stepped up and delivered a hard bonk to Wrinkle's shin, and Wrinkles yelped and grabbed his leg before toppling backward into the service shaft.

"I found the little bugger!" he shouted down the shaft, still grabbing at his ankle.

He was answered by an echoing shout. The crew was coming.

"Go!" Jonah said, waving the Space Raiders forward. "Leave him!"

He threw his bonker into his blanket and took off himself, scooping up Wrinkles's gun on the way. It felt heavy and awkward in his hand. He hoped he didn't have to use it.

Jonah sprinted down the Haunted Passage, sparing anxious looks behind them. The rest of Sector Three was close behind, with Alex taking the rear. They were about halfway down the hall when Red Eye stepped out of the service-shaft door where Wrinkles had been dispatched. There was no mistaking that fierce red eye or the gun that he aimed after the fleeing kids.

"Duck!" Jonah shouted, just as a blue blast fizzled down the hallway.

The beam shot straight over their heads and continued down the Haunted Passage.

"Keep going!" Jonah said.

Space Witch followed Red Eye out the door. They were in trouble now.

Jonah ran as fast as he could, whizzing past the air grates and the ripped-open gray door and Home Sweet Home. He ran past Sally's third most secret lair, and he spotted the ominous double steel doors of the Unknown Zone up ahead. What they would do when they got there he had no idea. He still didn't know where the Bubble was.

He needed Sally Malik.

He reached the control panel and punched in 111. The doors slid open, and he gestured for the others to keep running through. He could see Red Eye and Space Witch approaching in the distance. They weren't running. They just walked with cool, menacing confidence. They figured the Space Raiders would be trapped at the end of the hallway.

But when they saw that Jonah had opened the door, they broke into a run.

"Where now?" Lieutenant Gordon called from inside the Unknown Zone.

"Into the engine room!" Jonah said. "One-one-one!"

The last Space Raiders ran through the door. Alex stopped beside him.

"Is there a lock?" he asked Jonah frantically, his eyes on the pirates.

Jonah checked the control panel. "I don't think so. Just get to the—"

Alex stepped outside the doorway, lifting his bonker. There was a grim, determined look on his face. "Close it!"

"What are you doing?" Jonah asked.

"Smashing the panel," he said, looking back. Red Eye and Space Witch were almost there. "Close it!"

"Alex—"

"Close it!"

Jonah hesitated and then slapped the door panel. He saw a smile cross Alex's face as he pulled the bonker back and started to swing. The door slid shut just as a fizzling, smashing noise echoed down the Haunted Passage. He'd done it.

Jonah stood there for a moment. He thought about opening the door and trying to stun the two pirates. But if he did that, he would have wasted Alex's bravery.

Instead he turned and followed the other Space Raiders into the engine room. They were clumped together in a frightened heap, staring up at the tangled spiderweb of power lines and walkways and conduits, just as Jonah had done. But he knew they didn't have time to stand here. Red Eye and Space Witch would come in through the service shafts. And when they did, they would not be happy.

He looked around the engine room in desperation. There were so many openings and exits to the room, all bathed in shadows. He had no idea where to go.

"What did you do this time?" someone asked.

He looked up. Sally Malik was leaning over the walkway, shaking her head. Jonah had never been so happy to see someone in his life.

"We need your help," he said. "Where is the Bubble?"

She frowned. "Let me guess: The crew is coming to get you?"

"Pretty much," Jonah said.

"You're a real pain in my heinie," Sally said. "But you do keep things interesting. Start climbing. We're heading up."

"Of course," Jonah muttered.

The Space Raiders started up the service ladder, tucking their bonkers into their blankets and then awkwardly climbing with the bundles. It was a slow process, and Jonah kept anxiously looking at the service-shaft openings, expecting the pirates to come out at any moment. He wondered if Alex was okay.

The others had yet to notice he was gone.

Jonah was the last one up the ladder. By the time he reached the top, half the Space Raiders were already onto the next level. Willona hurried up to him.

"Where is Alex?" she whispered.

Jonah paused. "They got him."

Willona put her hand over her mouth.

"We'll rescue him," Jonah said. "Don't worry. Keep climbing."

She nodded and started up the ladder. Once again, Jonah was the last one up. He saw a few Space Raiders pointing down at the pile of bonkers and whispering as they waited to climb the next ladder.

"How much farther?" he called to Sally.

She poked her head over the next walkway. "This is it. If you Space Raiders could climb, we'd be there already."

Lieutenant Gordon glanced at her sourly as he scaled the ladder.

Jonah was halfway up when he heard the first shouts from below. Red Eye, Wrinkles, and Space Witch had come in through the service shafts. He could see them below through openings in the spiderweb. Red Eye was talking on a comm unit.

"Hurry up, space rat!" Sally called.

Space Witch was starting for a service ladder below him. Jonah climbed the ladder as fast as he dared, the bundled blanket swinging around behind him. He finally scurried out onto the fourth level, and Sally led the group in a dash across the walkway, heading for a service-shaft opening.

Jonah glanced down and caught a glimpse of Red Eye. He met eyes with the space pirate, and then Jonah plunged into the darkness of the service shaft.

Sally just kept running. She suddenly turned right, flinging open a door. The Space Raiders flooded through it, and Jonah found himself in another hallway identical to Squirrel Street. He slammed the door shut behind them.

"Almost there!" Sally said, already running down the hall.

Jonah and the others ran after her, all looking around curiously at the identical hallway. But they soon found a notable difference. A short hallway opened up to the right, which Sally turned and sprinted down. But instead of leading to another hallway, it only had one closed red door at the end with a smashed-in control panel on the wall beside it.

Jonah was just about to ask what they were doing here when Sally slid the door open with her hands and hurried inside. The Space Raiders followed her in, and then every single one of them stopped abruptly, their eyes wide. Jonah almost ran into them, and then he instantly saw why they had stopped.

The Bubble was a perfect name for the room. It extended out from the ship as a half circle. The floor was the same beaten gray metal as the rest of the *Squirrel*, but that was the only metal in the room. Thick glass extended from the edges of the floor back to the ship like a dome, revealing a magnificent view of space in front of and above them. Stars and nebulae and distant galaxies lit up the blackness like millions of candles.

Looking out, it was as if Jonah were floating in space. It was the most beautiful and terrifying thing he had ever seen. He took a quick step back, his hands finding the door. Many of the other Space Raiders did the same thing.

"Welcome to the Bubble," Sally said quietly. "My second-best hiding spot."

The Space Raiders took a while to settle in. They grouped

together in little clumps, sticking close to the ship and whispering to each other. Others just dropped their bundles and stood right next to the glass, staring out in silent amazement and barely listening to Lieutenants Gordon's orders to organize the supplies. Lyana the Forgotten was one of those. She just stood alone, less than a foot from the glass, and didn't move.

Jonah wondered what she was thinking about.

He made a little group with Willona, Jemma, Victoria, Matty, and Martin, laying out their blankets and sitting close for warmth. It was cold in the Bubble. He also informed Lieutenant Gordon of what had happened to Alex, and the lieutenant led the group in a memorial service.

"May he raid in peace," echoed around the Bubble for what seemed like hours.

Sally Malik sat alone in the corner, pressed right against the glass, and Jonah noticed she had a little bed set up there with a few extra blankets and pillows.

He wandered over and sat down next to her.

"How long have you used this place?" Jonah asked.

"Over a year," she said. "The door was open when I found it. The controls were already smashed, so I figured if I closed it, the crew would just assume they couldn't get in. Plus, I liked it here. It's one of my favorite sleeping spots."

"I can see why," Jonah said, watching the stars roll by. "I wonder why it's here."

Sally shrugged. "A lot of ships have observation decks. The passengers need a break from the cramped rooms and hallways. Probably has a control panel to keep them from camping out in here." She smiled. "Didn't work for me, I guess."

"Thank you," Jonah said. "You saved us."

"For now," she murmured, looking out at the group. "They're going to search the ship for you guys. They might not think to look here at first, but they will eventually."

"Yeah," Jonah said. "I know."

"Where is the commander?" she asked.

"Hiding on the second floor," Jonah said. "In the service shafts."

Sally nodded. "Doesn't surprise me. There are a lot of side tunnels in that area." She turned back to the window, hugging her knees to her chest. "What are you gonna do, Jonah the Now Incredible? How are you going to save your little friends?"

Jonah followed her gaze. "I have no idea."

CHAPTER TWENTY-TWO

JONAH BARELY SLEPT THAT NIGHT. HE WAS huddled next to Willona, who informed him that it didn't mean anything and that she hadn't forgotten his little kiss with Victoria.

It seemed to get colder and colder in the Bubble, and Jonah found himself shivering beneath his blanket. But it wasn't the cold that kept him awake. It was worry. Worry about what they would do next. And that wasn't all.

The Space Raiders all had their own rooms in the sectors, and so Jonah had just assumed they all slept soundly on the ship. That wasn't the case. Many of them murmured and spoke in their sleep, tossing and turning. Others woke up and walked around or stared out the glass. Lieutenant Gordon didn't even lie down.

Finally, Jonah sat up too, sitting against the wall with his knees pulled up to his chest and the blanket draped over his shoulders. Willona was murmuring something beside him, though she was smiling. At least she was in a happy place.

He noticed Victoria stir and look over at him. She pulled her blanket off and crept over to sit beside him, her shoulder pressed against his. Jonah felt his skin warm a little.

"Can't sleep?" she whispered, glancing at him.

"No. You either?"

She smiled vaguely. "I don't sleep much. Not since Matty was taken. Now it's just a habit, I guess." She brushed the hair from her eyes. "And if I couldn't sleep in my room, I definitely won't sleep in this place. It's beautiful, but even with all these people it feels lonely."

"Yeah," Jonah said. "I know what you mean."

She looked at him. "Tell me about your family."

"My family?"

"Yeah," she said. "I want to hear a nice story for once."

Jonah paused. "Well, my mom is a lawyer. She has the same hair as me, and green eyes, and she always wears gray suits. She looks very professional."

Victoria smiled. "And your dad?"

"He's a community planner. He's pretty serious. Doesn't laugh much. But when he does, it's this big, booming laugh that shakes the whole room. We never hugged or said 'I love you' or anything like that. But I think he did. I thought he did."

"What do you mean?" Victoria asked, frowning.

Jonah didn't say anything for a moment. He had this feeling that his voice might break or tears might well up or any number of other things that would be embarrassing. "I think they gave me up," he said quietly. "I think they sent me to be a Space Raider."

"Maybe it was a mistake," Victoria said.

Jonah stared out into space. "Maybe," he whispered. "I hope so."

"Any brothers or sisters?"

"Sister," Jonah said, smiling again. "Mara. Seventeen. She's really popular. She has an eighteen-year-old boyfriend who's the worst. He calls me Jonie."

Victoria snorted and then covered her mouth. "Sorry."

"It's all right," Jonah said. "Not sure why it bothered me, really."

"Things change on the *Squirrel*," Victoria said. "You see things differently."

Jonah looked at her. "Did you hate me when you found out I had parents?"

"No," she said. "I didn't hate you. But I didn't want you to be here. I wanted this to be a special mission for kids like Matty and me. I wanted to feel special. And at first you changed that a little. Like any kid could be a Space Raider. I thought we were here because we were strong. Because we had survived something terrible. It made sense."

"And now?" Jonah said.

She smiled. "Now I'm very happy you're here. I think you were a special recruit. Maybe you were sent here to lead the rest of us. I don't know. But you're a pretty good Space Raider, Jonah the Now Incredible. The best one ever, I think."

They met eyes. She really did have pretty eyes. Jonah realized they were going to kiss again. He wondered if she would move in. Should he? How did this work?

"Make me puke, why don't you?" Willona growled, standing up and yanking her blanket with her. "The best Space Raider ever? More like the . . . stupidest Space Raider ever!" She paused. "Okay, I didn't mean that. Don't tell Lieutenant Gordon. But still." She pointed a stern finger at him. "You shouldn't play with hearts. Not in space."

With that, she walked over to the next-closest group and lay down beside them, pointedly turning away from Jonah and grumbling something about charming spies.

"Maybe I should try to get back to sleep," Victoria said awkwardly.

"Okay," Jonah replied.

She quickly went back to the other side of the group and lay down, sparing Jonah one last smile before pulling her blanket up over her mouth. He sat there for a moment and then suddenly noticed that Sally was watching him from the corner.

She gave him a lopsided grin. "I've said it before, and I'll say it again. You are full of surprises, Jonah the Now Incredible. The space opera continues."

She turned back to the glass, chuckling and shaking her head.

Jonah sighed. Of all the problems he might have on the *Fantastic Flying Squirrel*, having two girls like him was far and away the most unexpected.

There was no day and night in space, of course, so the Space Raiders just woke and slept whenever they felt like it. They had breakfast, lunch, and dinner, which were organized under the watchful eye of Lyana the Forgotten, but other than that they just sat around and talked and slept and stared out the window. Hours felt like days.

Martin volunteered to take a message to the commander telling her where they were, and though Jonah tried to take his place, he refused.

"We need you here, Jonah," he said. "Just in case something happens. We need to use our special recruit wisely."

With that, he crept out and vanished down the hallway. He returned some time later and proudly boasted that he hadn't been detected by the crew or the Shrieker. He'd found the commander and the others by quietly calling out through the second-floor shafts. A small tunnel door had opened, and he'd been escorted by Erna the Strong to a very secret room where some power lines met at a small grid. Apparently they were very safe there, and the commander had sent a message for them to stay strong and be ready for the Dark Zone. This was met by smiles and purposeful nods in the Bubble.

The Space Raiders would be ready for their true mission.

Sally Malik came and went fairly regularly, sometimes disappearing for hours at a time. Whenever Jonah asked where she was going, she would just say that the Bubble was only her second-most secret lair and that she had business to attend to elsewhere.

Then she would give him a mock salute and disappear. Jonah just stopped asking.

He spent most of his time with Jemma. Victoria seemed too embarrassed to speak with him again, and Willona was deliberately avoiding him, though she did occasionally give him a dirty look. Jonah didn't mind. Jemma had a way of making him feel better, even if he was always half expecting Red Eye and Space Witch to burst through the door and arrest them all.

He also had several meetings with Lieutenant Gordon, who seemed at a loss as to what to do now. He didn't like waiting here without guard duties and food schedules and official meetings with the commander. But Jonah didn't have any answers for him.

He was just as lost.

At one point he wandered over to Ben the Brilliant, who was sitting with a group of his friends. He looked at Jonah in surprise.

"Yes?" he said.

"I just wanted to say thanks," Jonah said. "For saving my life. That was pretty brave. You're good with a bonker."

Ben's cheeks flushed just a little. "Well, it was nothing. Duty." He paused. "Next time move faster, curtain rod."

"See, I don't think that's an insult," Jonah said.

"Of course it is, you floating space rock."

Jonah shrugged. "All right. Well, thanks again."

"Yeah," he said, turning back to his friends. "Any time." He paused. "I mean last time. I mean I won't save you again. You owe me now."

Jonah just smiled and walked away.

The hours continued to roll by. The fourth-level hallway had bathrooms, so the only break anyone got from the Bubble was when they crept out in twos and threes to use them. The sleep shifts started becoming a little less restless in the Bubble as the Space Raiders got used to their new home, and even Jonah started to get a little sleep. His dreams were mostly filled with the Shrieker and EETs and Captain White Shark, but it was a start.

He was having a dream about shrieking monsters when Sally woke him.

"Jonah," she whispered. "Jonah!"

"What?" he said groggily.

"We have a problem," she said. "I was just in the

Haunted Passage. I heard shouts. Not the Shrieker. Space Raiders. Shouts for help."

Jonah quickly sat up. Most of the other Space Raiders were asleep. Lyana the Forgotten was watching them curiously from where she sat by the glass.

"Do you think—"

"They found them," she said grimly. "Definitely. I ran up here as fast as I could. I don't think we'll be able to save them this time, but if they found them, they're going to close in on the rest. Some might even talk. We need to tell the others before—"

She was interrupted by the loud crackling of the PA system. The Space Raiders all jerked awake, looking around in confusion. A commanding voice spoke.

It was Captain White Shark. And he sounded very pleased.

"Attention, passengers of my ship. Things have gone too far. You have shot a crew member. Destroyed a power line. Freed my prisoners. When I went to find the guilty parties, I learned that you had all run off and hidden on my ship. I was not impressed. My crew has been searching for you unsuccessfully, until now."

Jonah could almost hear him gloating.

"We have just captured forty-two of your little friends. I was only interested in my prisoners and in the fools who rescued them, Jonah Hillcrest in particular."

Everyone in the Bubble looked at Jonah. He tried to look brave.

"But now I've taken all of them. The brig will be very full," Captain White Shark said. "It will be very, very unpleasant. So here's the new plan. Bring me all my prisoners, and the leaders of your groups. All of them. At that time, I will release the others. I assure you, we will find all of you soon. But if you do not, and we do not find you, I will start eliminating prisoners one at a time. I want order on my ship. If that means blasting a few troublesome children into space to get it, then that's what I'll do."

Terrified murmurs filtered around the room. Even Sally looked afraid.

"And to my crew," the captain continued, "if you see Jonah Hillcrest, shoot him on sight. I repeat: Shoot him on sight. Make a choice, children. You have one day."

The announcement ended. Everyone was looking at Jonah again. Some looked like they might cry. Others were trembling. Some just looked like they couldn't move at all.

Jonah wasn't sure which one he was. He had been afraid. But this was different. Now the captain had ordered his crew to kill Jonah. He felt his hands shaking. But looking around, he knew they were waiting for him. Not Lieutenant Gordon. Jonah had been called out, and if he broke down, they all would. Jonah Hillcrest would have.

But not Jonah the Now Incredible.

He slowly stood up and looked over the room. His eyes fell on the lieutenant.

"Send a message to the commander," Jonah said quietly. "It's time to take over this ship."

CHAPTER TWENTY-THREE

THE BUBBLE FELL SILENT. JONAH LOOKED around, expecting a swell of pumping fists and salutes and cries of challenge. Instead he saw disbelief. Fear. Even scorn.

"That's impossible," Lieutenant Gordon said, shaking his head.

Jonah looked around the room. "Why? Has anyone tried?"

Ben snorted in derision. "His one little rescue has gone right to his head." He stood, staring at Jonah from across the Bubble. "How would we take over the ship? The crew has guns. You told us yourself: They're pirates. Criminals. They'd kill us all and ruin our mission. We have a job to do. And it's not get killed by space pirates, pig stink."

"Why do Space Raiders have to answer to a bunch of pirates?" Jonah asked, meeting his gaze. "We were sent to save the universe from the Entirely Evil Things from the Dark Zone. The crew has now threatened to kill us. Us. Space Raiders. They're the ones who declared war. We're just going to fight back. We don't need them."

Lieutenant Gordon was still shaking his head. He stood up and started pacing around the room, clearly agitated. "We don't even know how to pilot the ship."

"We'll learn," Jonah said. "If pirates can do it, so can we."

Ben threw his hands up in the air. "So, what . . . we just ask them to hand over the bridge? To lock themselves up and give us the ship?"

"No," Jonah said. "We take over the bridge and lock them up ourselves."

"He's crazy," Ben said. "He's got space madness!"

"I thought it was sadness?" Jonah asked, frowning.

"There's both," Willona murmured.

Jonah looked at his friends. Willona and Jemma looked uncertain. Afraid. Victoria was glancing at her brother uncertainly, though Matty looked determined. Martin the Marvelous looked like he was ready to go off to war that instant. He gave Jonah a grim nod.

And in the far corner, Sally Malik was just grinning and shaking her head, her arms folded across her chest. If anyone knew their chances, it was Sally Malik.

"Can it be done?" Jonah asked her.

Sally hesitated. "By me? No. By any Space Raider I've ever seen? No. But by Jonah the Now Incredible? Nothing surprises me anymore."

Everyone turned from her to Lieutenant Gordon. He was still pacing. "It can't be done," he said finally. "If it could have, the commander would have done it already." He hesitated. "I think."

"Well, this is her chance," Jonah said. "Just call a meeting. I'll do the rest."

Martin stepped forward. "I'm with Jonah."

"Me too," Willona said, "even though I hate him."

One by one, Space Raiders stepped forward. Victoria and Matty. Daniel the Ninja and Kyla the Courageous. Ria the Smart and even Eric the Excellent. Soon more than half had stepped forward. Lyana the Forgotten even joined him, though she refused to look Jonah in the eye. Ben looked around in shock as his friends stepped forward.

Jonah turned to Sally. She gave him a fleeting smile.

"Sorry, Jonah," she said. "I'm a space rat. I just survive."

Jonah nodded. He was disappointed, but he understood.

Lieutenant Gordon scanned over the room, counting the Space Raiders who had backed Jonah. When he finished, he met Jonah's eyes and nodded.

"Then there's no point in waiting. Martin the Marvelous . . . show us the way."

Jonah crawled through the cramped tunnel, led by Erna the Strong. Her dirty white sneakers were perilously close to his face. Behind him were Lieutenant Gordon,

Martin, and Willona. She'd asked to come along in case they needed an official announcement when they entered. He had a feeling she'd started to regret it as they snuck through the shadowy service shafts, following the fleet-footed Martin.

But they made it without incident, and now he had his chance.

Of course, now that he was crawling through the tunnel he had no idea what he was going to say. It was a little different from speaking with his sector. The commander terrified him, and he didn't have any friends in Sector One. They might just dismiss him, or even hand him over to the crew for being so foolish.

But he had to try.

Erna the Strong crawled out of the tunnel and stood up, though she didn't have a lot of headroom. A large, boxy power grid stood in the middle of the room, and power lines streamed into one side and poured out the other before continuing through a small opening to an adjoining room that looked identical to this one. But even with two rooms, it was packed and very warm.

Space Raiders were crammed into every square inch of the room, enough so that it must have been hard to lie down. With seventy members, Sector One was much bigger than the third sector, and they all looked very uncomfortable.

Jonah wondered if he might succeed after all.

His eyes fell on the commander. She was perched at the back of the room, surrounded by a tiny ring of personal space. Samantha was close by, and she gave Jonah a questioning smile as he walked in.

"Jonah the Now Incredible, Lieutenant Gordon," Erna the Strong started, and then paused. "And . . ."

Willona stepped forward. "Martin the Marvelous and Willona the Awesome."

The commander didn't stand up. Her hair looked a little clumpy and frayed, and her probing eyes were tired, with dark circles around them and heavy bags below.

"Why are you here?" she asked coolly. There was still authority in her voice.

Lieutenant Gordon stepped forward. "We would like to request a meeting."

Her green eyes flicked to him. "It seems you've already called one."

He paused, looking uncertain. "I didn't want to waste time."

The other Space Raiders were all watching very closely. Jonah saw some crawling through the opening from the other room, trying to get a look.

"Why do you want a meeting?" she asked.

"Actually, I do," Jonah said, stepping forward.

He had to avoid one Space Raider's leg.

The commander smiled, but it wasn't from amusement. "I should have known," she said. "What is it now, Jonah? What have you done this time?"

He met her eyes. "I want to take over the ship."

Just like the first time, the room fell into silence. Only the moaning, groaning engine could be heard, along with the buzzing of the power grid. He saw disbelief. Fear. But he only saw scorn on one face. It just happened to be the commander's.

She stared at him for a very long, very uncomfortable few seconds. Her finger tapped the metal floor beside her. "What is it you want, Jonah?" she asked finally.

He frowned. "What do you mean?"

"Are you trying to destroy us?" she said. "Is that your goal? Why? Why do you not want us to get to the Dark Zone? Why do you want to stop our mission?"

Jonah was taken aback. "I don't want to stop our mission."

The commander slowly stood up. "I think you do," she said. "You break every rule. You steal Lists. Attack crew members. Rescue prisoners. And now this."

Jonah saw Erna the Strong shifting beside him. She was ready to take him prisoner at a word from the commander. Martin took a small step beside him, putting himself between Erna and Jonah. Jonah bit back a smile. Martin barely came up to Erna's elbows. But Martin the Marvelous was a real Space Raider. And so was he.

Then it hit him. He knew how to win the crowd.

"Do you know why I did all that?" he said, looking around the room.

Everyone was looking at him. He had their attention.

"I did that because I'm a Space Raider," he continued, turning back to the commander. "I was chosen—like all of you—from the entire solar system to travel to the Dark Zone and save the universe. We didn't have a choice. We just woke up here with a mission, and we were all brave enough to accept it. We're all special. The most special kids in the solar system. And if I'm risking my life to save the universe, there's no way I'm taking orders from a bunch of smelly, miserable pirates. We're Space Raiders. We answer to no one."

As soon as he said it, Jonah knew he'd won. Lieutenant Gordon stood up a little straighter. Martin broke into a wide grin. Even Erna the Strong looked at him in amazement. But it was the crowd that showed the greatest change. Like a ripple in a pond, smiles and proud looks and hope filtered across the small, cramped room.

Samantha gave him a nod.

The commander saw it too. For the second time, she'd been bested by Jonah the Now Incredible. A strange look came over her face. It wasn't anger or resentment or even fear. It was sadness. A deep, tangible sadness.

"We've always done it this way," she said quietly.

"Then they won't expect it now," Jonah replied.

She still didn't want to agree. He could tell. She hesitated and looked around the room and hesitated some more. But she knew they all wanted to fight. Jonah suspected she could still stop it. If she gave the order, they would follow her. But maybe he'd stirred something in her as well. Something the commander had kept hidden behind those old eyes and tapping fingers and sweeping lightning-streaked locks. Because when she looked at him again, the sadness was gone. In its place was a grim determination.

"What's the plan, Jonah the Now Incredible?"

He smiled. "We act like Space Raiders. We march."

CHAPTER TWENTY-FOUR

A FEW HOURS LATER, JONAH WAS SITTING IN THE Bubble again, staring out into space. The plans were set. They weren't perfect, but it was the best they could do. He knew Space Raiders could be hurt. Maybe even killed. But he also knew they had to act. Something was wrong on the *Fantastic Flying Squirrel,* and he had a feeling they were all running out of time.

The deadline for Captain White Shark's ultimatum was the following morning, and that was when the Space Raiders would make their triumphant march on the crew's quarters. That meant they all had a long night ahead of them, waiting for a battle they hadn't expected.

He thought of the stars at home. He used to sit in his backyard sometimes with the patio lights off and stare up at space, wondering what secrets lay in the darkness. Now he was here, floating through them, and he still had no answers. Everything was big and dark and scary and lonely, and now all he wanted to see was the back door of his house, the light washing out from the windows, his parents sitting on the couch watching TV.

He wondered what they were doing now. If they missed him. He hoped so.

Jonah heard footsteps and turned to see Jemma sit down beside him. Most of the others were sleeping or talking quietly. Sally Malik was gone again.

"Hey," she said, smiling. Her bird's nest of straw-colored hair was even messier than usual, with strands falling out on all sides like she'd gone through a clothes dryer. "Just wanted to say congratulations."

Before they'd left, the commander had named him an official adventurer. The other assembled Space Raiders had all saluted happily as she said, "I give you Jonah the Now Incredible, Special Recruit and Adventurer of the Highest Order."

Willona had looked like she might cry.

"I greeted him, you know," she'd told a girl next to her.

Jemma smiled. "I also wanted to give you this."

She took a blue bundle out from behind her back and handed it to him. It was Jonah's school uniform, cut open and stitched into a square blanket. Jonah gingerly took it, blinking back an unexpected tear. It was strange to feel something from home again, and it made him realize just how far he'd come from the scared boy who used to put that blue uniform on and get pushed around at school. He put it close to his nose, smiling. It was comforting to smell his mom's favorite fabric softener as he stared out into space.

"Thanks, Jemma," he whispered, putting down the blanket.

"I'd thought I'd make you a special badge as well," she said, "you know, because you're the special recruit, but then I thought maybe that would be too much."

"Yeah," Jonah said. He looked down at his badge. "I'm happy with this one."

She paused and glanced at him. "Are you sure?"

Jonah frowned. "What do you mean?"

"Are you sure you want to do all this? You have a home to get back to. You could hide like Sally Malik until the *Squirrel* goes back to Earth."

"She's tried," Jonah said. "You can't get off the ship."

Jemma looked at him. "If anyone could, it would be you."

Jonah thought about that. There were probably ways. He could try to send a message to his family. Maybe sneak into the shuttle bay.

But he didn't want to run. He wanted answers.

"Would you go back, if you could?" he asked her.

"No," she said. "Although, I didn't mind Burbank Orphanage. There were about eighty kids there. A lot of their parents had died in the mines on Ganymede. That's where most people work. Good money, but very unstable under the ground. That's what happened to Martin's parents. He didn't like Burbank. He's very independent, as you can tell."

Jonah glanced at Martin, who was fast asleep in the corner. As usual he was lying flat on his back, his slender little arms and legs sprawled out, just as he was when Jonah thought he'd been shot in the brig. He really was a strange boy.

"I liked it, though," Jemma continued, tucking her sewing supplies back into her pocket. "Some of them made fun of me because of my scars. I guess you can expect that."

"How did you get them?" Jonah asked quietly.

She sighed and pulled back her sleeves. The scars ran all the way past her elbows. "When I was eight, we got in an accident. My parents and I. They crashed off the side of the highway, and the propulsion engine burst into flames. They came from below—burned most of my body." She lifted her pant legs. There were more scars. "The first responders managed to pull me out before the flames got to my face, but they were too late to save my parents." She looked out into space, the stars reflecting off her eyes. "That's when they put me in the Burbank Orphanage."

She pulled her sleeves down again.

"Like I said, some of the kids there were mean. But there was a worker there, a woman named Lolli, and she treated me like a daughter. She braided my hair and read me stories and did crafts. She was the one who always called me creative." She smiled sadly. "They took me while I was sleeping, I guess. I remember lying down, and then I was here. I wish I could have said thank you. I miss her. I called myself Jemma the Creative for her."

She turned to Jonah.

"But I would never go back. On Ganymede I was Jemma Main, another orphan. People don't adopt much on Ganymede. They came sometimes, though, and they'd say, poor little girl. What a shame." Her voice grew thick with emotion. "But here I'm a Space Raider. I have a mission. A uniform. No one says poor little girl, what a shame. They don't pity me here. Because I'm special. They chose me because I'm special. And for that, I would go fight Entirely Evil Things from the Dark Zone. And I'll definitely fight the crew."

Jonah nodded. "I understand."

"And what about you? Would you go back?"

Jonah thought about that for a moment. "I do like my uniform here."

Jemma laughed. "Thanks. There are boxes and boxes of them, you know. All different sizes. There's a big room in Sector One. We take boxes out and throw the old clothes in. There's a huge pile of old clothes. Six trips' worth, the most important uniform specialist said. That's what the commander told him. One thousand Space Raiders. You can imagine the pile."

"I thought this was the seventh trip to the Dark Zone?" Jonah said.

She paused. "I never thought about that. Must have made a mistake. Or maybe the first Space Raiders already had uniforms. Think we'll meet them in the Dark Zone?"

"I hope so," Jonah murmured.

Something was nagging at him. Sally Malik. Wearing her old purple sweater and ripped blue jeans and dirty shoes. Where was her uniform?

"Everything all right?" Jemma asked.

"Yeah," he said. "Just thinking."

She smiled and stood up. "I'll leave you alone. Try to get some sleep."

She crept back to her blanket and lay down, leaving Jonah to stare out the window again. He thought about what Jemma had said. About what this all meant to her. About what it meant to all of them. Without thinking, his hand found his badge, and he suddenly realized what it meant to him. Jonah the Now Incredible, Special Recruit and Adventurer of the Highest Order. He was a Space Raider. He wouldn't let them down.

But as he sat there, Jonah couldn't shake the feeling that something else was going on. And for the first time, he wondered if the answer might lie with Sally Malik.

When the Space Raiders woke up, Jonah forgot all about his questions. The day had come. Space Raiders folded up their blankets and brushed off their uniforms and rested their bonkers on their shoulders like ancient soldiers with rifles. They fell into two parallel lines, with Lieutenant Gordon standing at the front, looking brave and grim.

When the signal came, Sector Three was to meet up with Sector Two in the middle of Last Refuge Road, which ran just outside the Bubble, and together the two sectors would march on the main staircase to the crew's quarters, singing and shouting war cries and banging their bonkers like a true invading army. Jonah figured the crew would be there almost immediately. That's when things would get interesting.

"Ready?" Jonah asked Martin.

He nodded, wearing his typical grin. The gun they'd taken from Wrinkles was tucked into his belt, hanging down almost to his knee. "Ready."

They had their own mission. And everything relied on it.

He turned to Lieutenant Gordon. "Remember: as loud as you can."

"Understood," Lieutenant Gordon said. "Good luck."

"You too," Jonah said.

He looked out over the other Space Raiders. Willona and Jemma were huddled close together in line, looking nervous but determined. His eyes fell on Victoria. She was near the back with her brother, standing beside him.

She looked at Jonah and managed a weak smile. He gave her a reassuring grin.

"Oh, here we go," Willona muttered to Jemma.

Willona had taken off her broken glasses for the battle, though she'd still applied her bright red lipstick and tied her hair up in those wild porcupine bunches.

"We'll be back as soon as we can to help," Jonah said to the group. "But I'm sure the battle will be over by then. You're Space Raiders. They don't have a chance."

That brought new smiles to the group, and Willona suddenly stepped out of line and gave Jonah a firm hug.

"I can't stay mad at you," she said, her face pressed into his shoulder. "Try not to be killed, Jonah the Now Incredible. I can't stand any more heartbreak."

She released him, blushing a little and looking around the room, where many Space Raiders were raising their eyebrows, including Lieutenant Gordon.

"Anyway," she said, punching his arm, "have fun out there . . . buddy."

She hurried back into line.

"Okay," Jonah said awkwardly, "well, we should probably get going."

"Don't mess this up, space gas," Ben said.

Jonah sighed. "Still not an insult. Let's go, Martin."

He saluted. "Yes, sir!"

"You don't have to do that," Jonah said.

They slid open the door and hurried out, closing it behind them. Jonah had one last glimpse of the assembled Space Raiders waiting in formation. If he and Martin failed, they would all be imprisoned . . . or worse. He shut the door, trying not to think about it.

He and Martin jogged down the short hallway to Last Refuge Road, taking a quick look in either direction. Then they ran across the hall to the closest service-shaft door and started for the engine room, their eyes on the power lines over their heads.

"Think this is actually going to work?" Martin the Marvelous asked.

Jonah looked at him. "I really hope so."

CHAPTER TWENTY-FIVE

JONAH AND MARTIN HURRIED DOWN THE service shaft, listening carefully for shrieks and cackles. It occurred to him that the Shrieker had been strangely quiet lately.

He had a feeling that was a bad thing.

Of course, it was the Shrieker who had given him his plan. The only thing the crew hated more than Space Raiders was the Shrieker. He'd seen what had happened to Wrinkles and Weasel. The mere sound of the Shrieker had caused them to lose all sense and abandon their post, cursing and shouting and threatening. Weasel had eventually figured it out, of course, but it had served as a significant distraction.

And so Jonah's plan was an invasion of Shriekers. Fake ones.

When the signal came, the Space Raiders would march down Last Refuge Road in a heroic last stand. Or so the crew would think. They would emerge with guns drawn and order the Space Raiders to halt. At that point a string of adventurers would send a signal to Jonah and Martin, who would simultaneously kill the power to both the fourth level and the quarters, plunging everyone into complete darkness. Then the shrieking would start.

Sector One would sprint through both sections, shrieking and cackling, and while the crew was distracted, the rest of the Space Raiders would launch their assault, bonking knees and stomachs and whatever else they could get their hands on. The idea was that the crew couldn't shoot what they couldn't see.

At least that's how it was supposed to work.

Martin glanced at Jonah as they hurried down the service shaft. According to Lieutenant Gordon's chronometer, they only had about twenty minutes until the announcement. If they weren't in position by then, the Space Raiders would march right into the crew's hands. Jonah couldn't let that happen.

"What were you like at home?" Martin asked curiously, keeping his voice low. "You must have gone on lots of adventures. Were your parents adventurers?"

"Actually, I was a bit of a coward."

Martin laughed and shook his head. "Yeah, right."

"What about you?" Jonah asked, his eyes on the power lines.

Martin paused. "I was a bit of an adventurer, I guess," he said, almost sheepishly. He sighed. "I was a criminal.

A pickpocket. A classic bad kid. I didn't want to tell you. I thought you might think of less me. I mean, you did meet me in prison."

"How come you were a pickpocket?" Jonah asked as they kept moving quickly through the dimly lit service shaft.

"My parents died when I was five. I was an only child. I think I was always a bit . . . difficult. But when they died, I got put in Burbank, and I think maybe I got worse. I ran away eventually. Had no money or anything, obviously. So I started stealing."

He looked at Jonah, sounding embarrassed.

"I didn't think it was right. I was just good at it. That's why I was so surprised they took me into the Space Raiders. I've been trying my best since then. Minus the food bar. I couldn't help it—I like rats. We had a lot on Ganymede." He hesitated. "Do you think I'm a bad kid now? I shouldn't have said anything."

Jonah smiled. "I think you're a great Space Raider."

"Thanks," Martin said, standing a little straighter. "That means a lot coming from an Adventurer of the Highest Order. I won't let you down, sir."

"Stop calling me sir."

"Yes, sir," Martin said.

Jonah sighed.

They continued on in silence for a moment or two, and then Jonah heard it. Footsteps. He gestured for Martin to stop. The footsteps halted immediately.

"You hear that?" he mouthed.

Martin nodded. They both slowly turned but saw nothing behind them in the shadowy tunnel. They looked at each other and kept walking.

"We're being followed," Jonah whispered. "And I doubt it's a crew member. They'd just shoot us."

Martin's eyes widened. "Shrieker?"

"Maybe," he said quietly. "Be ready."

Martin's slender little fingers landed on the handle of the gun.

Jonah and Martin made it safely to the engine room, though Jonah heard footsteps several more times. Whatever was following them was very quick. He kept trying to turn and catch it, but with no luck. Once he saw what might have been a shadow stepping into a little nook, but he couldn't be sure. And they didn't have time to check.

They had to get into position. He just hoped the other adventurers didn't run into the Shrieker when they delivered their signal. The whole operation would fall apart.

They hurried out into the hanging walkway, and Jonah tried not to look down. The power line he had bonked the first time had been welded and fixed with a new steel casing. He'd have to do it all over again.

The power line to Last Refuge Road, the one they'd been following, streamed out through open air to the engine core. Martin would have to go down a level to bonk it.

They could shoot the power lines, of course, but Jonah was afraid they would permanently destroy them. Considering they hoped to take over the *Squirrel* when the attack was over, that would be a bad thing. Hopefully, if they just pierced the power lines, they could fix them like the crew members did.

"Remember, don't hold on to the bonker," Jonah said. "If it doesn't work . . . shoot it. We'll worry about it later."

Martin nodded. "See you on the other side."

He scurried down a service ladder. He made a good space rat.

"How long you think we have?" he called up.

"Ten minutes, maybe," Jonah said. "So be ready."

Jonah ran over to the other power line, bonker at the ready. He saw Martin reach his power line a level below him, and he nodded up at Jonah, holding the bonker with two hands. Now they just had to wait.

He felt his hands sweating as they gripped the bonker.

"I knew you'd come back," a familiar deep voice said.

Jonah slowly turned, his stomach knotting up. Red Eye walked around the walkway from the other side of the core, gun in hand. His bald head glinted in the stale light of the engine room, while his lips curled in a very evil-looking smile. But worst of all was that glowing red eye, fixed firmly on Jonah.

"The others searched the ship, but I waited," he said. "Wanted the double pay, you see. Make this trip a little more worthwhile. Now drop the pole. I could shoot you now, but I'd have to carry you all the way up. So just turn around and start walking."

Jonah hesitated. Where was Martin?

"I said drop it!" Red Eye said, aiming the gun.

Jonah was just letting it go when a blue flash whizzed by his head, missing Red Eye by at least five feet. But it was enough to cause Red Eye to turn sharply, extending his shooting arm and aiming below them. Jonah reacted instantly. He swung his bonker over his head and connected squarely with Red Eye's forearm.

The pirate howled and dropped his gun, which went clattering off the walkway and toward the distant engine-room floor.

"Nice one!" Martin called.

Red Eye clutched his right arm and stood up straight, causing Jonah to take a quick step backward. Why hadn't he done more bonker training? What was that move that Alex used? A spin? Jonah took another step backward.

"You just cost me some pay," Red Eye growled. "Now I'm going to be unfriendly." He snatched a comm unit off his belt. "Hilda. Engine room. Now."

He stepped toward Jonah, who quickly backed up again.

"Martin?" he called.

"I can't get a good shot!" Martin said. "Can he step to the right a little?"

"No," Red Eye said quietly, "he can't."

He suddenly lunged at Jonah, who tried to swing the bonker at Red Eye's other arm. Red Eye reached out and caught it, his grip like iron. With a flick of his wrist, he yanked the bonker from Jonah's hand and threw it off the walkway. Jonah heard it clang loudly off the floor a few seconds later.

"Now what, you little rat?" he asked cruelly.

"Uh-oh," Martin said from below.

Jonah looked down and saw Space Witch step out of the service shaft. Her pinched, flushed face was narrowed into a sneer.

"Take the other one!" Red Eye said.

"Run!" Jonah shouted.

Martin fired a fizzling blue blast, causing Space Witch to duck out of the way, and then Jonah heard him sprint down the walkway. Jonah decided to do something unexpected. He ran directly at Red Eye, who spreads his arms and legs to catch him.

But Jonah slid right through Red Eye's legs, and though he vainly tried to grab Jonah as he went through, Jonah hopped back onto his feet and kept running. He wasn't exactly sure where he could run to in the tangled spiderweb that was the engine room, but anything was better than letting Red Eye catch him.

He heard Red Eye starting after him, his boots clanging off the metal walkway.

Jonah rounded the massive core, catching a glimpse of Martin sliding down the rungs of a service ladder. Space Witch was already closing in.

Jonah slid to a stop. The walkway ran around to the other side of the core and then stopped at the far wall. There was no ladder on this side. There was nowhere to run.

He glanced back at Red Eye, who was walking toward him, wearing that evil grin again. Jonah had no choice. Taking a running start, he jumped for the core. There was only about a foot from the walkway to the core, but even that glimpse of open space below his feet was absolutely terrifying. He hit the top of the core, which was a flat, circular metal surface with a huge stream of wires running out the top, crouched, and started crawling for the other side. He knew they only had minutes until the signal came.

If they didn't turn off the power, the Space Raiders were doomed.

He glanced back and saw Red Eye hop onto the core. Jonah crawled faster, hoping that there was another walkway he could just drop onto on the other side. There wasn't. He reached the edge and found himself looking out over open space. Fifty feet below, Martin was busy climbing down onto the first level. Jonah pulled back.

He was trapped again. And Red Eye knew it.

The pirate walked slowly toward him. He must have

been at least six feet tall, tall enough that his head almost reached the ceiling. He smiled, revealing rotten teeth.

"That's enough now," he said. "I should throw you off and spare myself the trouble. But then we'd have a real mess, wouldn't we? Now step away from the edge. Let's get you back to the brig. Maybe we'll make some room for you," he added, smiling cruelly again. "We do need more space."

Jonah froze. He had failed everyone. Willona and Jemma and Victoria and even Lieutenant Gordon. They would all be captured. Maybe killed. He felt sick.

"Jonah!" Martin shouted from far below.

Jonah turned and caught a glimpse of Martin on the bottom floor, waving and standing in front of what looked like a computer console. The Space Witch was lying motionless on her back about twenty feet away, her gun beside her.

Red Eye looked over the edge. "You must be kidding me."

"Good news!" Martin shouted. "I can turn off the power!"

"Step away from that computer!" Red Eye ordered.

Martin laughed. "Or what? You'll spit on me?"

Red Eye grabbed Jonah. "I'll throw your friend off the core."

"Go ahead," Martin said. "He doesn't like climbing anyway."

Red Eye held Jonah over the side. Jonah looked down in terror.

"I mean it!" Red Eye said.

"Go ahead!" Martin replied.

"Martin . . . ," Jonah said.

At that exact moment, an adventurer ran out of the service shaft.

"Now!" he shouted, his voice echoing around the engine room.

Martin turned to the computer and typed something in.

"Stop it!" Red Eye commanded.

"Nah," Martin said.

Red Eye looked at Jonah. "You have bad friends."

Then he shoved Jonah off the core.

CHAPTER TWENTY-SIX

AS JONAH PLUMMETED TOWARD THE engineroom floor, he decided he had to agree with Red Eye. It was a strange thing, falling through the air. He whizzed past power lines and conduits and walkways, always just out of reach of his grasping, flailing hands. Panic took over, but for some reason he couldn't scream. The ground was getting very close.

And then something strange happened.

He felt his body slow dramatically. He was still heading downward, but in a strange, controlled fall, as if up were down and down were up. He felt as light as a feather as he coasted down past the first-level walkways, carried only by his momentum. He vaguely heard Red Eye shouting something far above. Jonah lightly hit the ground, bending his legs just a little and then standing. But even that motion sent him floating off the ground again. Martin, who was holding on to the computer console as his legs floated up behind him, turned to Jonah and grinned.

"Turned off the artificial gravity in the engine room," he said proudly. "Pretty cool, right?"

"Very cool," Jonah said, looking for something to grab on to.

He spotted Space Witch's limp body floating around nearby.

"How did you take her out?" Jonah asked.

"Played dead," Martin said. "Oldest trick in the book. When she walked over to scoop me up, I popped her with a stun shot."

Jonah shook his head in disbelief. "And how did you turn off the gravity?"

Martin plucked a little red computer key on a chain from the computer and pushed off toward Jonah, a gun tucked into his belt. He held up the key.

"Override key," he said. "Space Witch had it around her neck. Put this in and you don't need passwords, other than for the bridge." He reached Jonah and grabbed on to his shoulders. The two boys did a twisting turn in mid-air. "Also turned off all the lights in Last Refuge Road and the crew's quarters. The battle must be on."

Jonah nodded, feeling a bit queasy. "Then we better go help." He spotted Red Eye's gun floating around on the other side of the engine room. "Give me a push, will you?"

Martin and Jonah pushed each other, and Jonah went spinning toward the gun.

"This is awesome!" Martin shouted, heading right for a wall.

Jonah felt a bit nauseous, but it was pretty awesome.

His momentum slowly took him to the gun, and he grabbed it out of midair and looked up. Red Eye was rapidly pulling himself toward a service shaft. Jonah narrowed his eyes as he reached the far wall and kicked upward toward a walkway. Bonkers were floating everywhere.

Jonah reached the walkway and kicked off again. It was like swimming upward through the air. He pulled on conduits and power lines and kicked off walkways, all as Martin did the same thing on the other side.

"Probably could have turned the gravity on again," Martin called. "Wouldn't have been as fun, though."

Red Eye was almost to the service shaft. The adventurer must have retreated to the battle, because he was nowhere to be seen.

Jonah was up past the second level now, still flinging himself toward Red Eye. He was getting high up again, but heights were a different thing in zero gravity. Up and down and left and right didn't really matter. He aimed the gun toward the retreating Red Eye and fired. The blue blast crackled, missing the pirate by at least ten feet. Red Eye gave Jonah a very evil look as he finally reached the service shaft and disappeared down the tunnel. Jonah took a big kick off the third-level walkway, propelling himself toward the shaft. He couldn't let Red Eye get back to the others.

Even without a gun, he was dangerous.

Jonah grabbed the rail outside the service-shaft opening and looked down at Martin, who was close behind him. The smaller boy flung himself upward, and Jonah just grabbed his arm as he flew toward the ceiling.

Martin smiled. "Good catch."

The two boys pulled themselves along the walkway, toward the service shaft, and floated through the opening.

"I wonder what happens when we leave the—," Jonah started.

Without warning, gravity suddenly kicked in again and both boys fell face-first onto the hard metal floor. Jonah groaned and looked up.

"Makes sense," he muttered.

Martin rolled over. "My everything hurts."

Jonah spotted Red Eye sprinting down the shaft up ahead. "There he goes!"

The two boys scrambled back to their feet and took off after Red Eye. But the pirate was too fast for them, and he turned and bolted up the stairs to the crew's quarters.

"You help out on the fourth level," Jonah said. "I'll go after Red Eye."

Martin slid to a halt in front of the door to Last Refuge Road. "Good luck, sir!"

"Stop saying that!" Jonah called as he ran.

His sides were already burning with cramps. He never knew there was so much exercising in space. Jonah reached the staircase and sprinted up, the gun still feeling heavy and awkward in his right hand. He barreled through the open door to the quarters and ran out into darkness. He'd almost forgotten they'd turned off all the lights. He also realized there were no sounds of battle. He turned down the hall, squinting.

Where was everyone?

He was still peering down the hallway when a fist rammed into his stomach. It was like being punched with a battering ram. The gun spilled out of his hand and clattered to the floor, and he hit the ground right behind it, curling into a ball and groaning. He heard someone step beside him.

"Did you notice my eye?" Red Eye asked, a hint of amusement in his voice.

Jonah managed to look up. His scarlet eye was glowing.

"It's infrared, you idiot," he continued. "Darkness doesn't bother me at all."

He reached down and scooped Jonah up by the shirt, lifting him cleanly off the floor with one hand. He held Jonah close to his face, the stench of beer and beans thick on his warm breath. Jonah just hung there like a fish on a line.

"They called me, you know," Red Eye said. "Jake told me your little friends were marching toward the main stairs like an army of rats. He went down with

Lonn and Boggs while Tepper and Jones guarded your little friends. But I'm not an idiot, little boy. I knew you were coming for the power lines. You had to save your friends. So I told them all to grab a pair of infrared goggles before they went down. We have plenty on the ship, just in case the lights go out. Of course, you didn't blow the wire anyway. You just turned them off from the computer. Which makes it very easy to turn them back on."

With his free hand, he snatched the comm unit off his belt.

"Go ahead, bridge."

The lights suddenly flicked back on. Behind Red Eye, Jonah saw the Space Raiders from Sector One standing at the end of the hallway, with two crew members with goggles aiming guns directly at them. Two Space Raiders were lying still on the floor.

The commander was at the front of the group, and she met Jonah's eyes. He heard voices and then saw Weasel backing through the door from the main staircase, his gun aimed at Lieutenant Gordon and the rest of Sectors Two and Three, who followed him through the doorway.

Jonah felt his stomach, which had already been punched in by Red Eye, sink even farther. They had failed. He saw Willona slink in, her eyes downcast.

Even Martin came through the door, his gun gone. He saw Jonah hanging in Red Eye's grasp, and he looked like he might cry. More and more Space Raiders filtered in through the doors, escorted by gun-toting pirates. The crew members took off their goggles, laughing as the kids fell into a mass in the center of the hall.

"Did you really think you could beat us?" Red Eye whispered.

Then he punched Jonah in the stomach again, eliciting shouts and gasps from the assembled Space Raiders, and threw him toward the others. Jonah hit the ground hard.

He looked up and saw the terrified faces of the Space Raiders. He'd let them all down. That hurt more than the hard metal floor. It hurt more than a battering ram to the stomach. He met Willona's watering brown eyes. What would happen to them now?

The pirates spread out around the mass of Space Raiders, guns fixed on the group.

Jonah climbed to his feet as Red Eye walked toward him, comm unit in hand.

"We have them."

On cue, the bridge doors slid open, and Captain White Shark walked out. He fit his name perfectly. He was tall and lean, with a crisp black uniform that didn't match his ragtag crew at all. He walked with a professional, intimidating march, his cold gray eyes locked on Jonah. His hair was stark white and swept back, curling over with a slight edge like a fin. He stalked toward Jonah, who felt like a fish on a line again.

Captain White Shark stopped before Jonah, staring down at him. Then he looked out over the Space Raiders, pausing for just a moment on the commander. His face moved with a flicker of anger or disappointment or surprise. He turned back to Jonah.

"You've caused a lot of trouble, boy," he said quietly. "You all have." He looked at Red Eye. "Where is Hilda?"

Red Eye paused. "One of the boys shot her."

Captain White Shark narrowed his eyes. "Which boy?"

Red Eye looked over the gathered Space Raiders, almost one hundred and fifty of them, and then pointed right at Martin. "That one."

Martin swelled his chest, staring right at the captain. "And I'd do it again," he said. "Space Raiders answer to no one."

Captain White Shark stared at him for a long moment. "Dave."

Wrinkles suddenly broke into a grin and grabbed Martin by the shoulder, dragging him to the captain.

"No!" the commander said, stepping forward. "You can't—"

"I warned you all," the Captain said. "Again and again. My crew wanted to make an example of one of you, but I said no. Daren Elling was clear: None of the kids could die on board. So I held them back. And now you have attacked them again." He paused, still looking a bit uncertain. "That's enough. It's time to make an exception. We're a week away from our destination, and I will have no more issues. None. If you do not obey, I will kill another prisoner every day. Dave says you don't believe me. You will now." He looked at Wrinkles and nodded. "Do it."

Wrinkles smiled and pointed his gun at Martin's head. His finger flicked a switch. Jonah knew what that meant. He'd set the gun to kill.

Space Raiders cried out. He heard the commander shouting. Willona. Jemma. Even Erna the Strong. Jonah ran toward Martin, but Red Eye stepped up and threw him backward. He landed hard on his back, pain shooting through his body.

"Any last words?" Wrinkles asked.

Martin just stood there. He didn't even cry.

"May I raid in peace," he said proudly.

The captain looked away. "Now."

"I'd like to say something," a familiar voice said.

Jonah looked up. Sally Malik was standing in the service-shaft door, holding a gun and a bonker.

She saw Jonah and smiled. "I liked Jonah's plan. He's a dimwit, you see, but he had the right idea. Turn the lights off. But next time, don't just pretend to be Shriekers. Invite it along. It loves a good ambush. Jonah, I'd start with Red Eye."

With that, she threw the bonker to Jonah and fired

the gun right into the green power line that ran up beside the service-shaft door.

The lights flicked off, and everything plunged into chaos.

CHAPTER TWENTY-SEVEN

JONAH SCOOPED THE BONKER OFF THE FLOOR and sprang to his feet just as an earsplitting shriek filled the air. Everything was pitch black, but there was no mistaking the glowing red eye staring right at him. Sally was right. Jonah needed to take him out first. Of course, he still hadn't completed his bonker training. But he did know how to slide.

Jonah ran directly at Red Eye, and he knew the large man could see him coming. So when he was about three feet away, he slid feet first at Red Eye's legs, swinging the bonker wildly. He connected solidly with the pirate's right shin, and with a muffled curse Red Eye toppled over and slammed into the ground.

Jonah rolled away and stood up again.

The corridor was full of cackles and shrieks and shouting Space Raiders and cursing pirates. There was suddenly a blue flash, and Jonah caught a glimpse of a grinning Martin and a very surprised-looking Wrinkles falling backward as he took a stun shot to the chest. He also caught a glimpse of Space Raiders swarming over the pirates, punching and kicking and wrenching the guns from their hands.

Willona was right in the thick of it. She looked like she was biting Boggs in the leg. Jonah wasn't surprised.

But he also caught a brief glimpse of Weasel throwing a Space Raider off of him and raising his gun toward the crowd. Jonah gripped his bonker and charged.

He didn't make it.

As the corridor fell back into darkness, a strong hand reached out and gripped his ankle, sending him flying. He slammed into the floor once again but managed to hold on to his bonker. He had a feeling he was going to need it.

On instinct, Jonah rolled to the left just as a heavy boot slammed into the floor where his back had been. If he'd been hit, he might have been killed. Jonah swung the bonker at Red Eye's leg, but this time the big man stepped over it.

"Martin!" Jonah called. "The eye!"

But Red Eye was faster. He instantly switched off the red eye and became just as invisible as the rest of them.

"Where?" Martin called.

He fired down the hallway, and once again a strange scene lit up the room. Red Eye was standing directly over Jonah, looking huge and menacing in the eerie blue glow. Many of the pirates had been dispatched, held down by Space Raiders, and Erna the Strong was now engaged with Weasel, struggling over the gun. But the flash was enough that Red Eye spotted Jonah on the floor, and he lifted his filthy black boot to try to crush him again.

With another piercing shriek, Sally tackled him from behind, and Jonah just managed to roll out of the way as the light went out and the huge man hit the floor with a thud. He heard Sally scurry off before he could turn around.

"Martin!" Jonah called into the darkness.

"I got him," Martin said quietly. "Don't move, space trash, or I'll shoot."

Red Eye growled, and Jonah heard him try to lash out. That was a bad idea. Martin fired, and Jonah saw him wearing a crooked grin as the blue flash lit up the room. Red Eye slumped motionless on the floor, and the hall slipped back into darkness.

"You deserve a promotion," Jonah said.

"Thank you, sir," Martin replied proudly.

"Give me a break," Sally muttered. "Let me see if I can get the lights back on—"

She didn't need to. The double doors to the bridge suddenly slid open, shining light down the corridor. Captain White Shark was escaping to the bridge. He took one last look back, his cold gray eyes locked directly on Jonah, and started inside.

Jonah realized Captain White Shark could still lock

them out of the bridge. If he did that, the Space Raiders could never take over the *Squirrel*. Jonah gripped his bonker and sprinted after him.

"Space Raiders, charge!" Martin called, running after Jonah.

The Space Raiders took up the call and charged after them.

Captain White Shark made it inside and ran to the door panel. Jonah was still five feet away. If those doors closed, he knew they could never get them open again. Captain White Shark hit the panel, and Jonah dived. If he did one thing well, it was definitely sliding. He hit the floor and slid an extra foot or two, just enough that he managed to hold the bonker out with one hand and jam it in between the closing doors. They slammed into the bonker and groaned and strained but didn't close on the slightly bending metal pole.

He looked up and saw just the faintest hint of a smile cross Captain White Shark's face. Not a smile of happiness. It was a smile of complete and utter disbelief.

"No one can stop Jonah the Now Incredible!" Martin shouted, taking a flying leap over the bonker and into the bridge.

Captain White Shark might have been surprised, but he wasn't giving up. He lashed out with a boot just as Martin went airborne, catching the small boy right in the chest. He flew backward, slamming into the ground beside Jonah. He lay there for a second, staring up at the ceiling. Jonah scrambled over to him.

"Are you all right?" he asked.

"I'm just going to lie here for a second," he managed. "Get him for me."

Jonah nodded and scooped up Martin's gun. Then he charged through the doorway, sliding to a halt when he saw the empty bridge. It was incredible. A massive, sweeping window covered the front of the room, just like the Bubble, looking out onto a panoramic view of space. Control stations were situated around the room, including spots for the pilot and navigator, and stations on the wall for the communications specialist and lead engineer. But most impressive of all was the metallic gray-and-black chair in the middle of the room, raised on a large circular podium so that it overlooked the rest of the bridge.

He wondered what it was like to sit there.

At that moment, Captain White Shark popped over one of the control stations, gun in hand. Jonah threw himself to the floor just as a sizzling blue laser shot by right where his head had been and blasted into the far wall, just barely missing a control panel.

Crawling on his hands and knees, Jonah made a break for the nearest control station and flung himself behind it. He felt his hands sweating on the cool metal of the gun handle. He'd never even held a gun before today, and now he was in a gunfight in a room with a giant glass window covering half the wall.

This was not good.

He poked his head over the chair, and Captain White Shark fired again, being very careful to overshoot the equipment. As a result it sailed well over Jonah's head.

"Don't hit anything!" the captain shouted.

"So give up!" Jonah shouted back.

"This is my ship," he growled.

Jonah peeked out from the side of the black control station and saw that Captain White Shark was slowly making his way around the bridge, staying low. Jonah prepared to pop out and fire. He just had to avoid hitting the glass.

"Why are you even doing this?" Captain White Shark asked. "You're going home."

Jonah frowned. "What do you mean?"

"Did you think we were dropping you off too?" he asked scornfully. "The commission would have my head. Your parents have been asking too many questions."

"My parents?" Jonah said. He took another peek. The captain was getting closer. "Didn't they send me here?"

Captain White Shark snorted. "Send you? They've started an interplanet search for you! And they're starting to find clues, which Elling is not happy about. Why do you think Leppy is in the brig? He's the idiot who forgot Jonah Hillcrest the first time and made me go all the way back to Earth. And he's the same idiot who took you—Jonah L. Hillcrest—instead of the street rat Jonah R. Hillcrest who lives in the Charles Hodge Orphanage. He's lucky I didn't blast him into space. I still might, after all the trouble you've caused. By the time we found out, we'd wasted too much time. I told them I'd just drop the kids off and take you home after we were done. I expect Elling will meet with you first and explain what happens to your loved ones if you tell anyone where you've been."

Jonah's mind was reeling. He wasn't a Space Raider. He wasn't the special recruit. He was just a mistake. But that meant his parents hadn't given him up. The fact that they were fighting for him to come home meant they weren't sick of him. They really did love him. They really did want him.

But another part of him was suddenly afraid. Somewhere along the way he'd started to believe that he really was special. That he could do these incredible things.

But he wasn't. He was Jonah L. Hillcrest, regular boy.

The gun was trembling in his hands. He heard the captain's footsteps.

"I thought I'd leave you with the others," Captain White Shark continued. "We didn't want to take care of you. Clearly that was a mistake."

"I'm not a Space Raider," Jonah murmured.

The captain laughed. "No. And consider yourself

lucky. Now turn the gun over. I won't kill you, Jonah. I'd be tried for murder. Do it now and I won't kill your friends, either. Not that I need to. I'm sure PER-7 will take care of that."

Jonah perked up. Maybe he wasn't special. Maybe he wasn't a Space Raider. But he still believed something was wrong on the *Fantastic Flying Squirrel*. And there was only one way to protect his friends.

Jonah popped over the console and fired. Captain White Shark ducked out of the way, and the blue blast hit the glass and crackled across it with blue streaks and sparks.

"What is Project Weed?" Jonah shouted, firing again as the captain ducked behind another control station.

"How do you know about that?" Captain White Shark called.

"I found the folder," Jonah said, scurrying to another station. "What is it?"

The Captain peeked out and fired. "It's what your little friends are here for."

The blue blast just missed over Jonah's head, and he felt his hair stand up on end.

"Jonah!" Martin said, stepping through the door. "Did you get—"

He yelped as Captain White Shark fired at the door. Martin dove out of the way, covering his head with his arms.

"Guess not!" he shouted.

Jonah saw other Space Raiders crowding around the door. In a matter of moments, they would flood inside and the captain would be overwhelmed. He saw it too.

Captain White Shark sprinted for the door, obviously hoping to kick out the bonker and blow the panel, locking the others out. Jonah lifted his gun. He had one shot.

Jonah pulled the trigger, and a blue blast lanced out across the bridge. It wasn't perfect, but it worked. The blast hit the captain in his trailing leg, and he cried out and pitched forward as his leg went completely stiff. His gun spilled out a few feet in front of him. He tried to crawl for it, but Willona stepped in his way, pointing a gun at him.

"You've been space raided," she said quietly, and then looked at Jonah. "What do you think?"

Jonah smiled and stood up. "Not bad."

Martin hit the door panel, and the double doors slid open. The assembled Space Raiders, those who weren't guarding the downed pirates, streamed inside. At least a hundred of them crowded onto the bridge, and Captain White Shark pushed against the wall with his hands, unable to stand up. The commander walked in last, her green eyes immediately flicking to the captain. Her face visibly tightened.

Jonah walked across the bridge, gun in hand, and the other Space Raiders stepped aside to let him pass. He saw the admiration in their faces. He knew that wouldn't last long. When they found out he was a mistake, they would exile him again.

He stopped in front of the captain. Before that happened, he wanted answers.

"Where is this ship going?" he asked.

The captain scowled. "I told you. PER-7."

Jonah heard the other Space Raiders murmuring amongst themselves.

"What is that? Is it in the Dark Zone?"

He laughed quietly to himself. "No, it's not in the Dark Zone. It's Possible Earth Replacement Seven."

Jonah frowned. They were the seventh load of Space Raiders.

"What is Project Weed?" he asked again.

The Captain met his eyes. "I told you that, too. It's why they're all here."

"But what is it?" Jonah insisted. "What are the Space Raiders? What are they supposed to do? Why were they chosen?"

Captain White Shark sat there for a long moment, staring right at Jonah.

"Why don't you ask my daughter?" he said finally, shifting his eyes.

Everyone quickly followed his gaze. Before he even looked, Jonah knew.

He turned around and saw her pale cheeks flush

as the other Space Raiders stepped away from her in shock, forming a wide circle. She stared at the floor for a few seconds, and then the commander managed two mumbled words.

"I'm sorry."

CHAPTER TWENTY-EIGHT

THE TRIBUNAL WAS HELD ON THE BRIDGE. IT was one of the few rooms large enough to hold the entire assembled group of the Space Raiders, and it was still full to the brim.

There was a lot to do before the tribunal could be held. The power to the crew's quarters was restored by a closely watched Boggs, who used the welding equipment to fix the damaged power line. Of course, before the power was restored, they also had to free the captured prisoners from Sector Four and move the crew into the brig.

Jonah was the one to swing open the brig door and release them, and he was met by a saluting Alex the Adventurer. When Alex found out that Jonah had led a takeover of the *Squirrel*, he quickly took him aside.

"I owe you an apology," he said, his eyes on the floor.

"Why?" Jonah asked, confused.

"I was the one who attacked Grouter," he said quietly. "He chased me into a service shaft. He was right on my keister, so I jumped out and whacked him in the knee. It made a pop noise," he continued, wincing. "He fell into a lower shaft. I knew they would get me for it, so I hid for hours before I ran back to the sectors. Then, like a coward, I let you take the blame." He met Jonah's eyes. "I'm sorry, Jonah the Now Incredible."

Jonah smiled. "No problem, Alex the Adventurer. Friends?"

"I'd be honored," Alex said happily, saluting again. "You're the best Space Raider in history."

Jonah's smile had faltered, and he'd just saluted and gotten back to work. He wasn't looking forward to telling the others. He didn't have to, he supposed, but they had a right to know. Besides, he needed to get home. His parents were waiting.

When the power was restored and the crew—including Captain White Shark—were safely locked up in the brig and guarded by Eric the Excellent, the tribunal could finally begin.

Whispers and rumors were running through the ship, all directed at the silent sixteen-year-old girl sitting alone in the captain's chair, guarded by a grim-faced Erna the Strong. She had looked the most betrayed by the news, and she had immediately volunteered to guard the commander until the tribunal. Not that they needed a guard. The commander looked broken. Alone. Scared. Every time Jonah walked by, he just felt bad for her. Her fingers tapped the armrests.

But he wanted answers. And he knew she had them.

Jonah stood before the captain's chair, the Space Raiders assembled around him. The former lieutenants stood at his side, and behind them stood Willona, Martin, and the rest of Jonah's friends from Sector Three. The Space Raiders who had been hit by stun blasts were awake again, and though they were a bit groggy, they insisted on attending. Everyone wanted to hear the commander's story. They wanted to know why she had lied. Even Sally was there, standing by the door. She looked uncomfortable.

Jonah knew there were formalities and things he should say to start the tribunal. The commander always did. But he decided to just get to the point.

"Is it true?" he asked.

The commander kept tapping the armrest, faster than ever before. Finally, her tired green eyes found him through her lightning-streaked bangs. "Yes," she whispered.

The Space Raiders immediately started talking among themselves.

"Silence!" Lieutenant Potts called.

The crowd quieted again.

"How long have you lived on this ship?" Jonah asked.

She paused. "My whole life. I've never been off of it."

Jonah nodded. That explained her pale skin.

"Why are we all here?" Jonah asked.

Jonah saw tears start to dribble down the commander's face.

"You're here because of Project Weed," she murmured. "You're the seventh batch we've taken. We've already dropped off six other groups." Her voice faltered. "I didn't want him to do it. But we needed the money. They were shutting down the *Squirrel*."

Jonah saw the confused looks on everyone's faces. He knew it would get worse. Things were starting to click into place for him. And it wasn't good.

"What is Project Weed?"

She hesitated. "It's a top-secret commission project. Earth is too polluted. The ozone layer is collapsing." She was trembling. "They couldn't send the entire population to the other planets in our solar system. They couldn't put billions of people in domes. They needed new planets. Earth replacements."

She met Jonah's eyes.

"But the commission needed to know if humans could survive on the planets before they sent waves of people there. They don't know the planets well enough. If there are diseases. Weather patterns. Creatures." She paused again. "Intelligent life."

The Space Raiders were really whispering now. They looked scared.

"People weren't going to just volunteer," she said. "And so they decided to solve two problems at once." She looked behind Jonah. "There were too many orphans."

This caused the loudest stir yet. Jonah suspected many Space Raiders were starting to guess at the truth. But they believed the commander's story too much. They weren't there yet.

"They decided to send orphans to colonize the worlds. Two hundred at a time. One hundred boys. One hundred girls. They used young kids, and only two hundred, because they wanted to be able to take the worlds back if they wanted them. My dad told me if new settlers get comfortable, they stop taking orders. They fight for their homes. Kids wouldn't do that. They'd just be happy the adults had finally arrived. If they survived the first few years." Her voice cracked. "The *Squirrel* was going to be decommissioned. It was an old passenger ship. But Elling came to my dad and offered him the contract. He said our ship was perfect: No one would notice it was gone."

She looked out into space.

"My dad needed the money. He took on the contract and hired this filthy crew—pirates and mercenaries that he found in the old run-down dives by the spaceport. People who didn't mind abducting orphans and dropping them off across the galaxy. People that could keep them in line. And now we've been doing this for almost three years."

Jonah glanced behind him. He saw Willona watching

with shaking hands. Alex looking betrayed. Jemma looking scared. He wanted to stop asking questions. He wanted them to keep believing. But he couldn't.

They deserved to know.

"Did you make up the Incredible Space Raiders?" Jonah asked quietly.

The commander put her hands to her eyes, the tears streaming through her slender fingers. "Yes."

It finally hit home. He heard the gasps. The whimpers. The frightened voices.

"Why?"

The commander turned and looked right at Sally Malik. "The crew told the first batch what was happening. Where they were going. Sally was one of them. It was terrible. Kids cried and wept and begged to go home. They got angry and tried to take over the ship. One was killed. The rest were locked up until we got to PER-1. I remember the crying as they loaded them onto the shuttle," she whispered. "But one of them escaped. We'd become best friends, so I let her out of her cell. She hid on the ship, and she's been here ever since."

"The Shrieker," Jonah murmured, looking at Sally.

She flushed and looked away.

"Yes," the commander said softly. "I get to see her sometimes, but not much. Not while Space Raiders are on the ship. Sometimes I slip away, though, and Sally and I just sit in Home Sweet Home. When the Space Raiders are gone, we spend most of our time together. But we're never happy. We know where the others are going."

The commander shook her head.

"I begged my dad to stop the trips. But he wouldn't. So I made up a story. I wanted the kids to feel special. Like they'd been chosen for something important. They needed rules and uniforms and weapons. These big passenger ships always have boxes and boxes of emergency clothes, in case there's a disease outbreak. They sanitize everyone, burn their clothes, and give them these jumpers. The *Squirrel* never had an incident, so they were all still there. I also had bonkers. Those are just replacement parts for the core. They burn up all the time, so they keep thousands of extras. Sally agreed to make the noises and run around so no one would leave the sectors and go to the Unknown Zone. She knew what it was like to know the truth. And so she helped me cover it up."

"Why make up the story about the EETs?" Jonah asked. "Why not just say we were being sent to try to populate a new planet?"

"It was easier to keep an army in order," the commander said. "An army that had an enemy."

"Why were they chosen?" Jonah asked. "There are lots of orphans."

The commander paused and then looked at her feet. "They only chose orphans who ran away or caused trouble. Or ones nobody was adopting. The ones who stayed behind."

Jonah heard Willona sniffling. He saw tears in Jemma's eyes, and Martin's quivering lips. He knew it wasn't fear. Or even betrayal. It was that they all thought they'd been chosen to save the universe. That they all had a mission. It was like Jemma has said. They were tired of being pitied.

They wanted to be special. And the commander had taken that away.

The commander started shaking with silent tears. "I've already lied to five groups," she whispered. "I watched them get on the shuttles with their bonkers and head down to those planets. My father played along with it and ordered the crew to do the same. He didn't want any more trouble. And it worked. They saluted me as they left."

Her voice finally cracked, and she started to cry. Jonah met eyes with Sally Malik, who gave him a sad smile, as if to confirm the story. The tribunal was over. Everywhere Jonah looked, he saw scared children in old brown uniforms. The uniforms were too big. The badges were hastily made and stitched on. Their shoes, if they had them, were worn and dirty. Their hair was unkempt and greasy. Their eyes haunted.

They were orphans again. It had all come back. The pain they'd all faced. The loss they'd felt.

All they had wanted was a family. A purpose. And

now they were just crying kids in adult clothes.

But it was different for Jonah. He'd spent so much time being isolated and called a spy and wondering if he was here by mistake that he'd never quite believed he was a real Space Raider. Not like the others. But looking around, he finally understood what this was all about.

Jonah stepped forward. "I thought Space Raiders don't cry."

Everyone looked up at him. They looked angry. Like he was rubbing it in.

"There's no such thing as Space Raiders," Martin said quietly, standing at the front of the crowd. He looked like a little boy again.

"There *was* no such thing as Space Raiders," Jonah corrected. "There is now."

Martin frowned.

"We were all specially chosen," Jonah said. "Picked from the entire solar system. We have uniforms. Bonkers. Rules."

The commander was watching him now.

"What we didn't have was a ship," Jonah continued, gesturing around the Bridge. "We do now. We didn't have a mission. We do now."

"What mission?" Willona asked.

He turned to her. "To save the other Space Raiders, of course. To bring them all home."

"To Earth?" Alex said.

Jonah laughed. "Where are the Incredible Space Raiders from?"

"Space," the commander murmured, still watching Jonah.

He put his hands out. "Welcome home."

He saw the others look around. He saw the word "home" on their lips.

"Now," he continued, "who here is a Space Raider?"

There was a long moment of silence.

Then Martin stepped forward and saluted. "Martin the Marvelous, reporting for duty."

"Willona the Awesome," Willona said, saluting, "reporting for duty."

Like a tide, the rest of the Space Raiders shouted their names. Soon they were just shouting. Then they were high-fiving and laughing and jumping around. They were acting like kids. Willona wrapped Jonah in a fierce hug, burying her head into his shoulder. She pulled back and met his eyes.

"Thank you," she said.

He just nodded.

"Hold up!" Lieutenant Gordon said, stepping into the middle of the room. "There's one more thing we have to do. We need to name a new commander."

Lieutenant Potts swelled his chest. "Well, it should fall to the next in charge—"

"We'll have a vote," Lieutenant Gordon said curtly.

He turned and looked at Jonah. "I know who has my vote. If you want Jonah the Now Incredible, raise your hand."

There was no need for a second vote. Hands shot up everywhere. Erna the Strong raised hers instantly. So did Lyana the Forgotten. The only ones in the entire room who didn't were Ben the Brilliant and Lieutenant Potts, who looked around sourly. Even the commander raised her hand.

Lieutenant Gordon nodded. "Then I name Jonah the commander of the Incredible Space Raiders from Space, and the captain of the *Fantastic Flying Squirrel*!"

The cheer resounded through the bridge and down the hall. Countless hands reached out and shook Jonah's shoulders and patted his back and ruffled his hair. Victoria wrapped him in a tight hug and gave him a quick kiss, and they cheered even louder. It probably wasn't appropriate, but it was also one of the happiest moments of Jonah's life.

But as they cheered and shouted for Captain Jonah, he knew he had to tell them. He had to tell them that he was the wrong Jonah Hillcrest. That there was only one place he wanted to take the *Fantastic Flying Squirrel*.

Home.

CHAPTER TWENTY-NINE

JONAH SAT ALONE IN HIS OLD BEDROOM IN Sector Three, curled up on his bed and staring out the window. His journal was laid out on his lap.

When the celebrations had died down, Jonah had given out his first orders. The commander had been put in her bedroom in the crew's quarters and was guarded constantly by Erna the Strong. Jonah had mixed feelings about her. She had clearly been trying to save the orphans from further pain, but she'd also been assisting her father in taking them peacefully to the PER planets. Jonah was also afraid she might try to release her father from the brig, even though she swore she wouldn't. For now, locking her up was the best option. The other Space Raiders didn't have mixed feelings. They had been betrayed, and so they despised her.

His second order had been to name some new positions. He had named Alex as the new pilot of the *Squirrel*, Ria as the navigator, Martin as the new lead engineer, and Willona as the communications specialist. She had started crying when he'd given her the job. That was definitely another one of the happiest moments of Jonah's life.

His first officer was Lieutenant Gordon, while his other officers were Samantha, Lieutenant Potts, and Lieutenant Ebo. He figured they could help him assign other jobs to Space Raiders from the other sectors. Erna the Strong was, of course, the head of security, and Jemma was officially named ship tailor, at her request. The rest of the Space Raiders were assigned to security, bridge duty, engineering, maintenance, or food.

But first and foremost, they were all Space Raiders.

He also invited Sally to officially join the Space Raiders, and she accepted gladly, though she did inform Jonah that she refused to ever call him captain, sir, or commander. Jonah named her the official ship adviser. But after the commotion had settled, he pulled her aside. There was one more thing that didn't add up.

"Why did you go along with it?" Jonah asked her quietly.

Sally looked away. "Like she said: I was there. When Captain White Shark told everyone where we were going and why we were chosen, they panicked. It was awful. I remember everyone screaming and crying. When they tried to leave the sectors, the pirates beat them and shot them and locked them up. I had another friend here: Niraj."

Jonah frowned. That was the boy who had lived in his room.

"He tried again and again to get home. To take over the bridge or steal a shuttle or even to join the crew. He had younger sisters. He wanted to get back to them."

"What happened?"

For the first time since Jonah had met her, Sally's brown eyes started to water.

"They shot him," she whispered. "Right in front of us. After that, I realized there was no point fighting the crew. They were too strong. So when Sara let me out, I decided to just hide. I wanted to keep the new Space Raiders safe, so I came up with the idea of the Shrieker. We wanted to keep Space Raiders out of the halls. Sara came up with most of the rest, but I did help. I cried for days every time they took them down to those planets. I felt like I helped the captain. But I didn't know what to do."

She looked at Jonah.

"Until you came along and showed me we didn't have to be afraid." She turned away again. "I understand if you don't want me on your crew. I helped her lie."

Jonah paused. "I know why you did it. And you just saved our lives. You're a Space Raider now, Sally Malik. I'll have Jemma make you a uniform."

Sally smiled. "Thanks, Jonah."

When that was done, he'd asked for some time alone. Everyone had to start training for their new jobs, especially the bridge crew, so there was no rush. Jonah needed time to think. How could he tell them now that he wanted to go home?

He tried to write in his journal, but he didn't know what to say. He wanted to see his parents. He wanted to apologize for thinking they had given him away. He wanted to say all these things in person. But how could he leave?

A knock sounded at the door.

"Come in," Jonah said, putting the journal aside.

Willona smiled as she walked in and slid the door shut behind her. Then she plopped down on the bed.

"Hey," she said.

"Hey."

Willona looked at the window. "Feels like a long time ago that I woke you up in here, doesn't it?"

Jonah smiled. "Yeah. A lot has changed."

"But not everything," she said quietly. She was playing with her fingers in her lap. "Do you want to go home, Jonah?"

Jonah looked at her in surprise. "What?"

Willona rolled her eyes. "I know you better than anyone. You didn't come down here to take a nap. You want to go home."

He fell silent for a moment. "I don't know what to do."

"I know," Willona said. "But I just wanted to let you know that we're with you. If you want to go home, the Space Raiders will follow. We'll still come back for the others. But if you want to go home, we understand."

Jonah looked at her. "I guess I need to decide soon."

"Probably," she said. "Martin's already figured out how to make this thing fly."

"That doesn't surprise me," Jonah said. He thought about something and looked at her. "Where do you come from, Willona? Everyone else told me. What were your parents like?"

Willona shook her head. "Still breaking the rules. I come from space, Jonah. That's my home now. Where I come from doesn't matter at all." She paused. "But they were very nice," she said quietly. "I was an only child. They were very loving. They always told me I could be anything I wanted. That I just had to focus on my goals. That if I did that, I would be happy." She looked at Jonah. "When they died, I just wanted to be happy again. I wanted to be something great. And now I'm the communications specialist on the greatest ship in the fleet. I think my parents would be proud of me."

With that, she hurried out of the room, marching with her head held high.

Jonah smiled and leaned back. There was just one more person he had to talk to.

Erna the Strong stepped aside to let Jonah through the door, giving him a very professional salute as she did. Jonah had told everyone they didn't have to salute or call him sir, but some Space Raiders insisted on formalities.

Jonah walked inside, and the commander looked up from the corner. It was a nice bedroom. The cold gray walls were painted pink, and a frilly lace blanket lay over the cot. A desk with a computer sat beside it, along with a stack of journals.

The commander was sitting on the floor, her arms wrapped around her legs. Her eyes were puffy and red from tears, and her raven hair was matted to her cheeks and forehead. She looked like a little girl who had grown up too fast.

He'd realized it when he was talking to Sally. The commander had another name. She looked up, and her eyes widened when she saw what Jonah was holding. A tiny smile split her lips as he handed them to her.

"Mr. Monkey," she whispered, hugging the pink monkey to her chest. "And my notebook." She met his eyes. "I couldn't risk taking them to Sector One. How did you know?"

"It started adding up," Jonah said. "I realized you had to be the space princess."

"Thank you," she said. "My mom gave this to me. It's all I have left of her. When she passed away, everything started going wrong. They built new passenger ships and nobody wanted to fly on this old thing. My dad had put all his money into it, so we had nowhere else to go. I used to hear him crying after she died, shouting and screaming that he wanted her back. He did that for weeks. And then one day he just woke up, and he was cold. He wasn't my dad anymore. He was hired by the commission, and he found a new crew. Then we started picking up kids. He told me he was finding me some friends. He just didn't tell me what he was doing with them. Not until it was too late." She looked up at Jonah. "I'm sorry."

"I know," Jonah said, sitting down at the desk. "I need to ask you a question."

She nodded, still hugging Mr. Monkey.

"If I take the *Squirrel* back to Earth, what will happen to the Space Raiders?"

The commander thought about that for a moment. "The commission will send a team to take the ship back. They don't want the public to know about Project Weed, so they'll cover it up. The Space Raiders will be locked in the sectors and sent to PER-7."

"That's what I thought," Jonah murmured. "How many shuttles are there?"

"Two," she said, glancing at him. "One that could make it back."

"Could I fly it alone?" he asked.

"Yes." She met his eyes. "But you can't leave."

"Why not?"

She laughed. "Do you think this is over? The commission will send a ship to take the *Squirrel* back either way. Maybe pirates. Maybe soldiers. They can't have kids running around on a spaceship, especially ones who know a secret that the commission is trying to hide. They'll take the *Squirrel* back and send the Space Raiders to PER-7. The PER planets—we don't know what's on them. We don't know what you might find down there. And there are other things in space much worse than pirates. Trust me."

Jonah paused. "What happened that day?"

Her voice lowered. "They came fast. Attacked from the top level. Cut a hole in the ship. We were on a mapping expedition, looking for PER planets. My father and the crew fled down to the lower levels, trying to escape. Some of them didn't make it. Regular doors didn't stop them. We made it to the armory."

Jonah leaned forward. "Did you see them?"

"No," she whispered. "I just heard them."

Jonah nodded, the last piece of the puzzle falling into place. He'd wondered about the claw marks on the blue door and what was written in the diary. Part of her story was real.

"What happened then?"

"We stayed in there for two days. Finally, they decided to have a look. The creatures were gone. Their ship had taken off, and we've never seen them again." She looked at Jonah. "But they're out there, Jonah. The Entirely Evil Things. And this time there are two hundred kids on the *Squirrel*. It would be a lot worse. They need a captain. Someone who can lead them through all this. They need the special recruit."

"I'm not special—," Jonah started.

"Not because we had to go back for you," she said. "I knew it was a mistake. But you're special because you have a family. You don't need this like the others do. It made you question everything. And it made you fight back. You can't leave them, Jonah."

Jonah looked into her piercing green eyes, and he knew she was telling the truth. The thought of evil creatures roaming the stars was enough to make his skin crawl. But she was right. He couldn't leave them. Not yet.

Not until the other Space Raiders were safe.

"Is there a way to send a message back to Earth?" he asked quietly.

She nodded. "We're out of range of a broadcast, but there are a few message pods in one of the storerooms. You can send one back to Earth."

"Thanks," Jonah said. "Well, I better get back to the bridge."

"Can I ask you a favor?"

"Sure."

She looked down at Mr. Monkey. "My father isn't evil. He's just . . . broken. My mom is dead. I've barely even spoken to him since this started. I think he feels alone. I'm not excusing what he did. I hate him for it. But he's still my dad." She glanced at Jonah and handed him the pink monkey. "Can you give him this? He knows my mom gave it to me. Just tell him that I still love him and it's not too late."

Jonah took the monkey. "I can do that."

"Thank you."

"In a week or two I'll talk to the others about letting you out."

"No rush," she murmured. "I have some writing to do."

Jonah smiled and headed for the door. "Me too."

Dear Mom and Dad and Mara,

I wrote you a bunch of letters on this ship, but I figure one will probably do. I guess you know what happened by now, but if not, I kind of took over the Squirrel. It's a long story, but I'm a captain now, and we have to save the other Space Raiders.

Actually, none of this makes any sense without the other letters. Doesn't matter.

What's important is that I can't come home. Not yet. I want to, but it doesn't feel right abandoning my friends. I'm not the same scared little boy who left. Well, I'm still scared. And a boy. And I haven't grown, at least not physically. But everything else has changed. And I think that's a good thing. I would like to grow taller still. A few inches, even.

Anyway, there are a few things I wanted to say. The first is that I love you. I know I accused you of possibly giving me away—actually, you wouldn't have known that. Ignore that last sentence. But I know now you missed me, and I also know that I am very, very lucky to have parents like you. And you, too, Mara. Still not your boyfriend, though.

The second thing is that I will come home eventually. I don't know when, but I'll come back. And don't worry, I'll be fine. I'm pretty good with a bonker. Long story.

Finally, I need you to do me a favor. There's a boy living in the Charles Hodge Orphanage named Jonah R. Hillcrest. He was supposed to be here, but they took me by mistake. I think he would have liked it here. I think he would have found a home.

I'd still like him to have one. I know this is a lot to ask, but could you look after him until I get back? He can have my stuff. Sorry if he's a pickpocket or something, but it turns out pickpockets aren't half bad either. Give him a chance. He'll probably surprise you.

Well, I better get to the bridge. We're about to set out for PER-I to save the first batch of Space Raiders. I've never captained a ship, as you know, so wish me luck.

And if this is the last letter you get from me (even though I said I'll be back), good-bye. I love you. If strange men come to the door for the new Jonah, tell him to hide.

Sincerely,
Captain Jonah the Now Incredible,
Commander of the Incredible Space Raiders from Space

Jonah read over the letter one last time and then stuffed it into the circular message pod and closed the cap. It was time. He'd given Captain White Shark the monkey and the commander's message—accompanied by two Space Raiders with guns, of course—and watched as he took it with trembling hands. When Jonah closed the brig door, he thought he saw tears in Captain White Shark's cold gray eyes.

He walked down the crew's quarters toward the bridge, where the double doors were wide open. Space Raiders saluted him as he walked by. He walked onto the bridge, where his crew was waiting. Martin was standing by the wall equipment.

"Do you know where we blast off message pods?" he asked.

Martin nodded. "Of course."

Jonah tossed him the pod, and he caught it in both hands. "Please send this when you have a chance. To Earth."

Martin grinned. "Yes, sir."

"I told you to stop—" He sighed. "Thank you."

Jonah climbed up into the captain's chair and sat down. It was big and bulky and his feet didn't even touch the floor, but it was still quite a view. He looked into space, where a million stars and nebulae and planets sparkled in the darkness. It was beautiful.

"Did you find PER-1?" Jonah asked Ria, the new navigator.

He'd debated which group to save first, but they'd ultimately decided to go for the group that had been stuck on the planet longest. It seemed fair.

"Yes, sir," Ria said, glancing back. "Two weeks' flight."

"I guess we better get started," Jonah said. "Alex, let's go bring the Space Raiders home."

Alex grinned and pulled the throttle. With a slow, steady movement, the ship started forward. The bridge crew cheered—Willona being the loudest—and Jonah heard the cheer echo back through the hall, where it was taken up by the other Space Raiders.

He knew there was danger ahead. He knew this journey was far from over. But no matter what happened, they'd already won. Because not one of these Space Raiders was an orphan anymore. A castoff. They were a family, and this was a home. There was no better feeling than that. And for now, it was his home too.

He was Jonah the Now Incredible . . . from Space.

ACKNOWLEDGMENTS

Thank you to my new and yet already long-suffering wife, Juliana, who puts up with me while I voyage across the stars. Your patience and humor give me a great reason to come back to Earth. Thanks as always to my parents, who still support and encourage me every step of the way, even though I don't have to live at home anymore and eat all their groceries. Sometimes I wish I still could, though. Thanks to the rest of my family for your love and support, and a special mention to my first nephew, Jacob King—you're not even one yet, and you're already in a book! I hope you like this one day.

Thank you as well to Deb and Rick for bringing me into your family with open arms. Rick, you're an inspiration to anyone facing challenges in their life, and you certainly put my problems in perspective. I'm honored to call you my father-in-law.

A huge thank-you to my fantastic editor Sylvie Frank, who shares a love of all things wacky and weird and fun. You brought humanity to the story, so thank you. And thank you as well to Paula Wiseman for bringing me on board and giving this strange story a chance. And, of course, to my amazing agent and friend Brianne Johnson, who continues to provide me with support and encouragement. Thank you for continuing to believe in me and for always pushing me to be better.

And thank you to the rest of my extended family and friends. You all went out and bought my first book and showed up at signings and continue to support me every day. I can't express how much I appreciate that.

Finally, I just want to share a note about the dedication. My cousin passed away while I was writing this book, but she left behind a legacy of compassion, adventure, and pure joy that will be sorely missed. The Samantha in this book appeared before that tragic news, but I think she shares the same spirit of adventure. Sometimes the little things we do in life make the biggest impact on those around us. For her, it was just a smile.

THE BRIDGE
THE QUARTE
THE WILD ZONES
THE HAUNT
PASSAGE
THE SECTORS